Somerflip

Copyright © 2015 by Daley James Francis
www.DaleyJFrancis.com

Cover Design © 2015 Peter O'Connor
www.BespokeBookCovers.com

All rights reserved. This book or any portion thereof may not be reproduced or used in any manner whatsoever without the express written permission of the author except for the use of brief quotations in a book review

The right of Daley James Francis to be identified as the author of this work has been asserted in accordance with the Copyright, Designs & Patents Act 1988

All characters in this novel are fictitious. Any resemblance to actual events, locales or persons, living or dead, is entirely coincidental

ISBN 978-1508729754

About the author

Daley James Francis has been writing stories since he was a kid. The only things that have changed over time is his spelling and the size of his beard.

He has been a freelance writer since graduating from De Montfort University with a degree in Creative Writing and Journalism in 2012, and in that time, has written for many publications, written and produced short films that have been shown in festivals all over the world, and watched a life-threatening number of episodes of The Wright Stuff.

He lives in Loughborough in the United Kingdom, with his wife and addiction to Netflix.

And on the street tonight, an old man plays
With newspaper cuttings of his glory days

- Manic Street Preachers,
If You Tolerate This Your Children Will Be Next

1

The first stone skimmed across the surface of the water with effortless grace. The second hit the surface and sank without trace.

"I counted six bounces," said Rob Thomas, a smile on his face as he considered what effect his achievement would have on his competitor, who didn't even manage one.

"You don't count the final one. That doesn't count," replied Liam Thomas, a nine year old boy with less meat on his bones than a small turkey in a household of fatties on Christmas Day.

Father and son couldn't have been more different. Rob was a behemoth of a man. Six feet six inches tall and two hundred and fifty pounds of solid muscle, the majority of it around the shoulders. He was twenty-seven years of age, but could've been mistaken for a thirty-five year old bodybuilder.

Liam had inherited his mother's eyes and fair hair, and was a beautiful looking kid. It hurt Rob to see how handsome he was, as he had a face like sledgehammered meat, which he in turn had inherited from his father. The term 'British bulldog' could have been created for Rob, but he must've done something right to have won the heart of his wife, Faye, and to have created the wonderful little fella that had accompanied him to the reservoir.

Liam's head dropped over his miserable attempt at skimming stones on the water, and Rob ruffled his hair. It annoyed Rob that his own hair was short, fuzzy and black, and when it grew past Grade 4 it looked like a bog brush, whereas Liam's hair looked like David Beckham's circa 1998. You could fire a tsunami in its direction and it would still look catwalk ready.

"Practice makes perfect, buddy," Rob said, reassuringly. "I've got twenty-one years' practice over you."

"One day I'm going to hit a seven," Liam said.

"Yeah you will."

Every Saturday morning, Rob would take Liam out for a walk. It had become a weekly ritual that had started before Liam could even crawl, and over the last nine years, Liam had gone from holding daddy's hand to taking baby steps, and then to chasing rabbits.

When he was around six or seven, Liam would moan about having to go, and would huff and puff as he put his hat, scarf and gloves on. Now that he was older, Liam looked forward to his weekly wander with Dad, as he barely got to see him in the week. Rob worked long hours at the factory, which left him tired and unsociable when he came home.

By the time Rob had eaten and wound down after work, Liam was ready for bed, and as much as he tried to fight it so he could spend time with his dad, he was out for the count by 8pm and wouldn't make a peep until dawn.

It was around 8am on a cool October morning, and the reservoir looked like an illustration from a Jane Austen novel. Mist was clearing from the water, and the large country houses on the other side looked stunning as sunlight broke through the clouds behind them. Rob and Liam had seen four other walkers on their hour-long trek, and the beauty of solitude meant that the wildlife felt free to pop up and take a look around.

Rabbits were chasing each other in and out of the hedgerows, and a gang of geese had congregated by the water, accompanied by a scattering of ducks and swans, which were sitting on the surface. Liam kept an eye on the rabbits as they ducked and dived out of view every few seconds.

"Lots of rabbits, Dad," he said.

"Hundreds of the bleeders," Rob replied.

"I do like rabbits."

"They're OK in small doses, but you rarely get them in those."

"Because they reproduce so much?"

Liam's question made Rob chuckle. "Yeah, I guess so," he replied.

"Ben told me that he heard his sister Emma say 'he went like a rabbit'. Is that a metaphor?"

Rob put his head down and used the top of his zipped-up jacket to hide his mouth, as he was grinning his head off. He composed himself before answering.

"You're full of the big words of the world today, aren't you?" he asked. "I think you call that an 'analogy'."

Liam nodded along in agreement. "I'll look it up," he said.

"I bet you will. I wouldn't repeat that Emma line to your mum though. Not unless you want to go to bed without any tea tonight."

"I won't. I can't imagine she would find it very funny."

Liam giggled. He didn't understand his own joke, but he liked that he was amusing his dad.

They strolled down the man-made trail along the shore until they came across a bench. Liam had made it his weekly task to read the dedications on them. He liked discovering how long the people had lived for, and found the maths trickier when the person had died in this century.

Rob let out a sigh as he sat down on the bench. Liam read the plaque.

"Gordon Taylor. 1978 to 2013," Liam said, before whispering numbers to himself as he did the maths.

"He was thirty-five when he died?" Liam said, looking up at his dad for reassurance.

Rob leant over and read the shiny new plaque. "Yep. What an age to go," he said.

"Did you know him?" Liam asked.

"No."

"Oh."

Liam ran his finger around the lettering as he pondered the idea of being dead at thirty-five.

"I'd like to have a bench when I die," he said.

Rob pointed over to the geese, as a few of them took flight, and Liam bolted upright to watch. He stood and watched open-mouthed as they flew off in unison. Rob's plan had worked. It was too early in the morning to be discussing mortality with a nine year old boy.

It wasn't long until something else was on his mind.

"Dad?"

"Yes, kiddo?"

"Are swans and ducks related?"

Rob paused, frowned, and let his mouth gawp open.

He was stumped.

"I don't think so. I'm not really sure."

"They've got a similar head, but that's about it. But if cats and lions are related, I don't see why ducks and swans can't be?"

"I love ducks," Rob replied, taking the decision to keep the subject light.

"Me too," Liam said, breaking into a beaming smile.

"I love it when they fly across the water and then skid to a halt," Rob continued. "It looks like fun. I think a duck has the look of an animal that knows what its strengths and weaknesses are, and they just get on with it."

Liam took his father's words in, then nodded in agreement. He gazed out over the water, where the mist had all but cleared, and jumped down from the bench to pick up a stone. He approached the water's edge and threw it.

Two bounces and a kerplunk.

A gobsmacked Liam spun around and faced his father, who was applauding his son's new-found skimming prowess. Rob cupped his hands around his mouth and used them to imitate a roaring crowd, and Liam did a little on-the-spot victory jig, before punching the air like the final shot from a Rocky film.

"Good shot buddy," Rob said.

"Thank you, thank you," Liam replied, taking three bows to his audience of one before being distracted by the ducks that had mistook the stone for bread.

"No bread for you, ducky-poos," he said, which was met by a chorus of quacks. Liam watched the ducks swim by.

"Do you think the swans here lord it over the ducks?"

"I think the reservoir is probably a multicultural society," Rob replied, hardly containing a smile.

"So they live together in harmony?" Liam asked.

"I'd like to think so."

"Me too."

"Unless somebody throws in loads of really nice bread. That probably starts World War Three."

"If swans and ducks had World War One and Two?"

"You're right. They probably sat on the fence during the first two."

"Or on the water."

"Huh?" Rob was caught out by that one, which brought Liam a few seconds of joy.

"They would sit on the water, not the fence."

"Oh right. Yeah, I guess they would." Rob broke into a huge smile. "I love the way your mind works."

"What do you mean?" Liam asked.

Rob shrugged his shoulders.

"I just do," he said, bashfully.

Liam kicked a couple of stones through the short grass into the water.

"I wrote a story at school the other day," he said.

"Was it about the duck and swan war?" Rob laughed.

"No. It was about Grandma and her adventures in Australia."

Rob's smile vanished, and he fidgeted in his seat.

"Oh really. What was the story about?" he asked.

"She's been emailing Mum about stuff. I stole something she said and turned it into a story."

"You wouldn't be the first person to do that. What was it about?"

"It was about a koala called Lily."

"That's sweet. It would be rude not to hear it then. The stage is yours."

Liam cleared his throat, which brought the smile back to Rob's face. Liam stood in front of his father and prepared himself, like a great actor preparing to perform an Alan Bennett monologue at the Royal Court.

"Lily is a young koala. She lives in a eucalyptus tree and sleeps all day long, except when she's eating leaves and cuddling her mum. One day, she is woken by the smell of burning. She opens her sleepy eyes to see that she is surrounded by smoke. She climbs down, looking for her friends and family as she does. But she's all alone and can't see anything because of the smoke. She walks along until the grass becomes a harder, more painful surface. The smoke begins to clear, and Lily realises she is standing alone on a road."

As Liam told his story, an astonished Rob was becoming more and more impressed by his storytelling prowess. He was engrossed in his tale.

"Only, she doesn't know it's a road, so she keeps walking. The next thing she hears is a strange screaming sound and a loud screech. A car had swerved out of her way and smashed into a long pole. Lily's eyes gazed up the pole, and she saw a yellow sign with a picture of a koala on it. She decided it might be a good idea not to walk on the hard painful surface anymore, so she went back to the grass. Her home was burning down, but she decided that finding a new place to live would be better than dodging cars. She saw her family and friends doing the same thing, and joined them on their journey."

Liam paused for a moment, posing like a true storyteller.

"The end," he said, before taking a bow.

Rob was silent, but Liam could see that he was impressed.

"That's my story," he said.

Rob exhaled like he had been punched in the gut, then leant forward to give his verdict.

"That's an amazing story," he said, and Liam broke into a smile as wide as the reservoir. "Where did you get that from?"

"It was in an email that Grandma sent to Mum. We read it together, and she printed it off for me so I could rewrite it."

"So your version was different?"

"Yeah, I had to change it. The email was from Grandma's perspective."

"What happened in Grandma's story?" Rob asked.

"In Grandma's email, she and Roy were driving along in his Jeep, and they passed a forest fire. Grandma noticed that the road next to the burning field had the bodies of seven dead koalas in it. Grandma said it was the saddest thing she ever saw because there were signs everywhere, warning drivers that koalas and kangaroos will be crossing the roads. Grandma got upset and Roy started laughing. He told her that it was the norm in Australia, and that kangaroos and koalas being killed was good because it kept the numbers down."

"I believe that's called a 'cull'," Rob said. "But I don't think being hit by cars has anything to do with it."

"He said that kangaroos are a nightmare because they reproduce a lot."

"They're at it like rabbits," Rob said, in an attempt to lighten the mood after the harrowing story.

Liam chuckled slightly, then threw another skimmer. This time, the stone collapsed into the water with no bounce at all. Liam wiped his hand on his jacket and sighed.

"I'm getting bored now," he said, turning to his dad, who could see that Liam was getting frustrated.

"OK. Let's go back to the car," Rob said. He stood up and stretched out, and looked over to the family of geese that arrived at the shore.

"Look, the boys are back in town," he said, nodding over to them in an effort to shake Liam out of his irritation.

Liam looked over to the geese and back in a millisecond, murmuring a disinterested 'uh-huh' as he started to walk away from the water and back to the walking trail. Rob put a comforting arm around him.

"You did really well to see it from the koala's side. That was really impressive," he said.

"Thanks, Dad," Liam replied.

"Don't think about it so much. Your mum will think I've put you in a grump."

"What's for dinner?" Liam asked, his mood slowly recovering.

"You think with your belly, like your dad."

"I'm a growing boy."

Liam showed his dad his guns, tensing his biceps as hard as he could. Rob laughed and grabbed them, squeezing them and then pulling his arms behind his back. Liam started giggling as he tried to break free, but he was no match for his beast of a father.

"Argh, get off!" Liam yelled, albeit through giggles. Rob let go of his arms and kicked him up the backside, and Liam windmilled his arms back into circulation and straightened out his waterproof jacket.

"You've got a lot of growing up to do before you can beat your old man in a fight," Rob said.

"One day," Liam said, shadow boxing as they walked the trail. "One day."

"How about some chips for tea?" Rob asked.

"And fishcakes?" Liam replied, excitedly.

"If you want fishcakes."

"Yup."

"Then fishcakes you shall have. Great food for wimps."

Rob kicked Liam up the bum again. Liam turned and charged his dad, who picked him up and roughed him up. When your dad has hands that are larger than most people's heads, picking a fight with him is a bad idea – especially when you're nine years old.

"I'm going to leave you here with the swans and geese," Rob said, holding a giggling Liam above his head.

"HEY-HO!" A male voice boomed from behind the pair.

Rob carefully placed Liam back on his feet, and he turned to see who was shouting at them from down the trail. The sun was in Rob's eyes, but not Liam's. He could see that it was Jamie Sampson, an old school friend of his father's, who would regularly take Rob out drinking at the weekend. Jamie's hair was thinning fast, and he resembled a meatball due to his short arms and legs, which had earned him the nickname 'Jamie DeVito' from his pub mates.

Jamie was accompanied by his son Carl, a brat with a buzz cut whose face had a permanent sneer. Arms folded and constantly looking for trouble, Carl was the only kid at Liam's school who had been suspended from school, and he had been visited by the police on more than one occasion. This had led to him being labelled as the toughest kid in class, despite the fact that he was a thief and an arsonist, not a fighter. Jamie struggled with the walk, and Carl shuffled alongside him with a face like thunder, in his signature arms-folded stance. He nodded to Liam as they approached, and Jamie and Rob shook hands.

"Ey-up fatty, how's it going?" Rob asked.

"Don't you start," Jamie said, desperately trying to get his breath back. "I've had this one whingeing at me the whole walk."

Rob looked down at the little grump. "Alright, Carl?"

"Yeah," Carl said.

"Miserable toerag," Jamie chimed in.

"Hi, Carl. How are you?" Liam asked his school friend.

"I'd be a lot better if I wasn't here."

Carl left his father's side, grabbing Liam's coat and dragging him away from the adults and down to the water's edge. Rob and Jamie watched them go.

"Don't be long you two," Rob called out.

Jamie took a Jack Daniel's hip flask out of his coat pocket.

"Wanna bit?" Jamie asked, holding it out.

Rob shook his head and waved it away. "I'm good, pal. Cheers."

"I need this to put up with that little bastard. He hid my walking boots this morning. I found them outside in the dog kennel. I told him, 'Do that again, and you'll be sleeping in there permanently'. He called me something under his breath and went and got his gear on. I swear to God, sometimes I wish I'd just had a wank the day he was conceived."

"Bloody hell, Jamie."

"Nah, not really. He's alright," Jamie took three big gulps from the hip flask, then smacked his lips and purred like a house cat. "That's some sexy shit right there."

"Did you go out last night?" Rob asked.

"Oh yes, and you missed a cracker," Jamie said, perking up instantly.

"Really?" Rob said, with genuine surprise in his voice. "What happened?"

"Turns out Robyn Drever has been screwing her husband's sister's fiancé," Jamie said, causing Rob to work through the family puzzle in his mind.

"That's confusing," he said. "Husband. Sister. Fiancé. Jeez, that's a bit close to home isn't it?"

"Just slightly. The fiancé's had trials for Leicester Tigers, man. He makes you look like Rick Moranis. Anyways, he turns up at the pub and Robyn's there with her husband, who's the only person in the pub who doesn't know she's banging the rugger player. You could've cut the atmosphere with a knife."

"Ah, man. Feel for the bastard. What happened?"

"The fiancé comes over and gives Robyn a kiss on the cheek, and offers to buy them both a drink, and something just washes over the husband's face. He's fucking twigged it, and when he looks around the room and sees all of these faces looking at him, he stands up, grabs an empty bottle from the table next to him and smashes it on the side of the fiancé's watermelon of a head."

Rob flinched and pulled a face like he had been flicked in the balls. "It was weird, mate," Jamie continued. The fiancé didn't even flinch. It was like he knew he deserved it. He nodded to the husband – who, by the way, was visibly shitting his pants waiting for the reaction – and turned to everybody in the pub to apologise for the commotion. And that's when we noticed the ear."

"The ear?" Rob said, half-smiling and half-wishing that he hadn't asked.

"It was hanging off, mate. I mean it was just disgusting. Flapping around like Carl's little dick in the wind. He didn't even notice."

Rob put his hand to his mouth, then covered his face with both hands. Jamie started to laugh and pulled Rob's hands away from his face so he could continue telling the story with maximum dramatic effect.

"Robyn threw up all over the table, and Mick jumped over the bar and took the fiancé outside and called for an ambulance," Jamie said, before pausing for the final part of the story. "Now what would you do if that was you and Faye?"

"I'd be thinking of Van Gogh jokes to use at family get-togethers."

"Seriously, you dick," Jamie said, playfully pushing Rob's shoulder.

"I'd get out the pub for starters," Rob said.

Jamie shook his head.

"Nope," he said. "They moved to another table and carried on like nothing had ever happened."

Rob took a deep breath, then exhaled. "This fucking town, man."

"I know. It was so weird in the pub after that. Everybody was treading on glass for the rest of the night, not to mention egg shells, waiting for something to kick off again. You could hear it crunching on the soles of your shoes."

"What happened to the fiancé?" Rob asked.

"Dunno. I guess he got stitched up. Can you imagine the shit-storm that's coming in that household though? 'Oh hello sweetie, why's your ear off?' 'I've been shagging your brother's wife. How about some Findus Crispy Pancakes for tea?' Doesn't bear thinking about."

"Faye and I have a pretty boring marriage by the sounds of it."

"If that's boring, I'd say stick with it, pal."

"Hear, hear."

"Ear, ear."

They both sniggered.

Liam sat on the bench, and Carl honked up all the mucus he could muster and spat it on the ground next to it. Liam scrunched his face up at the sound of it. Carl kicked a stone, then leapt up on the bench and sat on the top, his muddy boots ensuring that nobody else would be sitting on it for a while.

"This is absolute bollocks," Carl declared.

"What is?" Liam asked.

"What d'ya mean, 'what is'? Have you not seen where we are? I could be eating Shreddies right now, or Weetabix and warm milk. But no, I'm walking around in the freezing cold with my fat dad. He makes me go on these stupid walks with him, but he doesn't even talk. He just sweats, huffs and puffs, and keeps pissing in hedges. And now I'm sat on a gay bench staring at ducks."

"I love ducks," Liam said.

"Ducks are gay," Carl fired back.

"Ducks aren't gay."

"Ducks are gay and all swans are arrogant," he declared, adamant that nobody would be right about anything except for him today.

Liam shook his head and focused his attention on the water in a bid to ignore Carl's nonsense. Carl looked between his legs and spotted Gordon's plaque.

"What kind of a bellend has a bench named after him?" Carl said, before spitting on the ground in front of him.

"A man who died," Liam said.

Carl didn't answer. He just stared at the two swans that were floating by.

"I'm going to have a street named after me when I die," he proclaimed.

Liam put his hands in his pockets to keep warm and dragged his foot through the gravel. He could only stand Carl for so long, and in this foul mood, his patience for him was stretched even further. Kids like Carl bored Liam, and for good reason. Unless you were into stealing, fighting or causing trouble, he wasn't a lot of fun to be around.

Carl grew restless, jumped off the bench and picked up the nearest stone. He dusted off the mud and showed it to Liam.

"I think I could take a swan out with a stone," Carl said.

"You can't do that!" Liam said, his voice going up a pitch.

"Why not?" Carl asked, and held his arm by his side, ready to throw.

"Because it's cruel," Liam said. "And I think swans are protected."

Carl laughed and pushed Liam with his free hand.

"With what? An invisible force field? My arse, protected. Watch this for a swan-shot."

Carl took a short run-up and threw the stone at the swans. Liam squirmed as the stone made its way towards the beautiful, majestic white birds.

The stone missed. It smashed into the surface of the water, an inch away from one of the swans' heads. The birds squawked and flapped their wings furiously, arching their backs up in anger.

Carl reacted like a centre forward who had just missed a penalty. He looked up to the heavens and cursed the gods for his failure.

"Bastard!" he yelled.

Liam wanted the ground to open up and swallow him whole.

"Did you see that?" Carl said, jabbing Liam's chest with his fist. "That swan ducked."

Carl's unintentional pun sunk in, and he burst out laughing. He jabbed Liam a few more times.

"That's brilliant, that! 'That swan ducked'. Geddit? Don't you think that's funny?"

Silence.

Carl resorted back to his original foul mood in an instant.

"You're as gay as these ducks," he said.

Liam took the wise decision to rejoin his dad, in the hope that it would spur him on to take him away from Carl and his plans of swan homicide. Carl followed, spitting three more times on the way back to the trail.

Jamie was finishing off another story from his night out as the boys arrived.

"I won't talk about it much in front of the boys, but he went down like his bones had been removed. Limp as a priest's cock. Then we bought a kebab."

Rob had never been happier to see his son return. It was as if they'd spoken telepathically to each other, and the message was: Let's get the hell out of here.

Liam rested his head against his father's hip. Rob put his arm around him and pulled him closer, rubbing his arm to warm him up.

"Alright, buddy?" he asked. Liam nodded.

For Jamie, witnessing such a close bond between father and son was a melancholy sight. It was something he didn't have with Carl. All they did was wind each other up. Carl had his sneer back, and stood at arm's distance. Jamie shook his head at him and turned to Rob.

"He'd rather be in bed, playing with his winky or getting his mum to make him Marmite on toast. But he needs to get out and get some exercise or he'll end up like his dad," he said, giving Carl a disapproving look.

Carl dropped his head and kicked some gravel.

"Don't be too hard on yourself, Jamie," Rob said. "It took you nearly thirty years to get like that."

"It's not too late to turn it around," Jamie said. "I'm starting at the new gym soon. They've got a sauna and steam room, too. Gotta make sure I don't sit in the sauna for an hour then drink four pints. That's what usually happens."

"I'm sure you'll be fine," Rob said.

"We need to train your metabolism now while you're young, lad. That means regular exercise and healthy eating."

Carl looked up at his dad, who was now pointing a finger at him whilst judging him with a complete lack of irony.

"I could be eating Shreddies now," Carl said, his voice turning whiney.

"With all the sugar you put on them? You'll have black teeth or no teeth at all. Your mum's twenty-eight and her mouth's got more fillings than Mr Kipling's pies."

Rob could see that the tension between the pair was anything but playful banter, and tried to change the subject.

"The boy just likes to come up here and watch the ducks," he said.

Jamie thought this was sweet. Carl mouthed the word 'gay' in Liam's direction, and Liam's eyes narrowed and his fists clenched.

"You're lucky you don't have to try so hard, Rob," Jamie said. He cleared his throat and slapped Carl around the back of the head, prompting an 'oww' and a look that could kill. "Right then, let's get you home."

"See you later, Jamie. You too, Carl. Look after your old man, eh?"

Carl shrugged his shoulders and blew a raspberry.

"He loves me really," Jamie joked. "See you later. Take care now, Liam. Good lad."

Jamie and Carl walked ahead, and Rob held Liam back so they wouldn't have to endure Carl's whingeing and Jamie's idle threats.

"And don't think I didn't see you peg that stone at that swan," they heard Jamie say. "If you have to throw stones at anything, aim for a duck."

The apple rarely falls far from the tree.

Once Jamie and Carl were a safe distance away, Rob put his arm around Liam and led him along the trail.

"Are you cold?" he asked.

"No. I'm fine. I think Carl was looking for ways to get his dad to take him home. I don't think he likes it here."

"I think you're right."

"At least the swans are safe now," Liam observed, which brought a belly laugh from Rob.

"Yeah," he laughed. "They'll be fine."

Liam stopped suddenly in his path. He turned to the swans, geese and ducks that were now returning to the human-free zone around the shore, and waved.

"Goodbye, ducks. Goodbye, geese," Liam yelled. Rob stopped and watched, a grin etched across his face. "Goodbye swans, too."

They continued down the trail. Liam caught sight of their red Peugeot 308, which was his cue to race his dad to the car. He sprinted as fast as he could, with Rob giving him a head start. But when you're a kid going up against a man as tall as Rob, a head start means nothing. Once Rob decided to give chase, the race was as good as over.

Liam stretched out his arm to touch the car and win the race, when suddenly a hairy hand, followed by a giant arm, pushed out in front and touched the car first.

"You beat me again!" he yelled, in mock anger.

"You'll beat me one day," Rob said, ushering Liam into the passenger seat as he got his breath back.

They drove out of the car park and onto the main road.

"Hey, Dad?" Liam asked.

"Yes buddy."

"That story Carl's dad was telling you. What was it about?"

Rob sighed a little as he searched for the right response.

"The same as always. Nothing as interesting as your stories, and never as brilliantly told."

2

Faye Thomas took advantage of the ninety minutes of peace she was afforded on a Saturday morning by deep cleaning the house. A huge Manic Street Preachers fan, she had created her own Nicky Wire-inspired T-shirt to do the cleaning in, with the words 'I Love Hoovering' spray-painted on it.

Faye had been a heartbreaker at secondary school, where she and Rob first met at eleven years of age. She had resembled a young Stevie Nicks, with shaggy dirty-blonde hair and the biggest blue eyes you'd ever seen. She terrified the nice boys and bewildered the rebellious types, as she looked and behaved like she didn't give a damn about anything. Rob was infatuated with her from day one, and he pursued her for three years before she finally gave in. They were the definition of childhood sweethearts.

Their home was a modest three-bedroom end-terrace, and by the side of the house there was a small patch of green where the local kids met up to play football. Unfortunately, the kids used the wall as their goal, so there would often be entire afternoons when all the Thomases could hear were the repetitive sounds of a ball hitting against the wall, followed by a few seconds of cheering.

Friends and family wondered how they had remained sane, to which they replied that it was nothing compared to living five doors away from a railway line for three years, and that they had got to the point where they would keep score and place bets with each other on who was going to win. They said that if they hadn't found a way to deal with these things, they'd have gone mad by now, and it seemed to have done the trick.

Faye was playing music as she hoovered, and despite the fact that she couldn't hear anything over the machine, she sang along. 'Hallelujah' by Alexandra Burke was playing, and Faye mumbled the bits of the song she didn't know until she got to the 'hallelujahs'. The combined sounds of Ms Burke, Mrs Thomas and the hoover drowned out the sound of Rob and Liam returning. They kicked off their muddy shoes and left them at the back door. They sneaked through the kitchen and peered through the glass door at Faye, who was deep into the song.

Liam looked up at his dad, and Rob gestured for him to be quiet as he tiptoed into the living room and unplugged the hoover from the wall socket, just as Faye was in full warble.

"Halleluj-*huh*?" she said, spinning round to see what was going on.

Rob stood with the plug in his hand.

"You're a horrible person," Faye said, embarrassed.

"Some people would say that I'm merciful," Rob said.

Faye marched over and snatched the plug out of his hand. She could hear Liam giggling from inside the kitchen door.

"What are you finding so amusing?" she said, frowning whilst trying to contain a smile. Liam shrugged his shoulders and looked at his dad for support.

"How can you hear anything with that hoover blasting?" Rob asked. "Actually, I understand now. It drains out the sound of Jeff Buckley turning in his grave."

Faye playfully slapped Rob on the arm, before turning the music off and packing the hoover away. Liam and Rob joined her in the living room and plonked themselves down on the sofa. Faye put her hands on her hips and didn't look too impressed with them.

"Excuse me, I've just cleaned this house. I don't want you two stinking out the place."

"It looks lovely, Mum," Liam said, which made Rob smile.

"It does," Rob said.

Faye decided to change the subject.

"So, how was your walk, young man?" she asked.

"It was nice. We saw ducks, geese and swans. Tons of rabbits," Liam replied.

"Aw, that's sweet. I love rabbits. Not keen on swans though. They always seem so full of themselves."

"I don't think these ones will be full of anything but a fear of stones," Rob said, confusing Faye.

"Huh?"

"We saw Jamie and little Carl up there. Carl was bored so he threw a stone at a swan."

"I'm surprised Jamie made it up there without having a heart attack," she said.

"He was knackered. Still had enough puff in him to compose a historical re-enactment of the latest punch-up outside the pub though."

"Urgh, that place. They should torch it, with everybody inside!"

Rob frowned at Faye and nodded down at Liam, as if to warn her.

"I mean it!" Faye said, ignoring the warning.

"Not in front of the boy, yeah?" Rob muttered under his breath. Liam was too busy yawning and flicking through the TV channels to care much for anything they were talking about.

Faye wasn't done yet.

"I would happily march Liam down there and pay for ringside seats," she said, rather theatrically. "I'd hold his chin so he couldn't take his eyes off it. Hell, I'd make him wear the headgear from *A Clockwork Orange* if it meant that it would sink in and he'd never go there in his life."

"He's not going to go there in his life. For a start, he's got more than two brain cells, which is three more than I've ever had."

Liam broke away from channel surfing to take issue with Rob's analogy.

"That sentence didn't make any sense," he said.

"I'm just exaggerating. Now put Sky Sports News on."

Liam screwed his face up. He'd choose cartoons over sport every time.

Faye was determined that she was going to get her point across.

"What your father means is that you have the potential to do something very good with your life, which doesn't involve drinking and fighting your life away like the majority of this town."

Liam shrugged his shoulders and settled for *Ben 10*, much to Rob's frustration. He didn't understand his mum's concerns about the town's drinking establishments, and right now he didn't care.

"Are you going out tonight?" Faye asked.

"Yeah, just for a couple," Rob replied.

"With Jamie?"

"He might be there. It's a free country."

"And you're a free bodyguard, protecting mouth almighty from his due comeuppance."

Rob sighed.

"I think you're taking this a little too seriously," he said.

Faye folded her arms and raised an eyebrow.

"Please. Not in front of the boy."

Suddenly, Liam leapt out of his seat and marched into the kitchen. Faye and Rob listened and, as soon as they heard the fridge open, knew that it was safe to talk again. They continued their discussion in a harsh whisper.

"Can you stop talking about the pub, Jamie and fighting?" asked Rob.

"It needs to be said. We need to get this through to him at an early age."

"Not after we've been for a walk and he's watching cartoons."

"It was on that walk that Jamie's little shitbag nearly decapitated a swan, remember?"

"OK. I take your point. But don't worry about Liam, he's not going to be like Carl."

"I sincerely hope not. Can you please be careful with Jamie tonight? He's a homing beacon for trouble, and it's always you who has to save him. As long as you're around him, he won't care who he starts on. He knows nobody around here can beat you."

Rob let out a laugh, then held out his hand to apologise.

"I'm sorry, I shouldn't've laughed," he said. "Have you been watching *Rocky V* this morning?"

Rob stood up and approached Faye, placing his hands on her arms and rubbing them. He bent down and looked into her eyes, which was tough with Faye being a foot shorter than him.

"All it takes is some quiet footsteps behind me and a plank of wood, or a perfectly timed punch from somebody who knows how to punch, and I'm out like a light. It's that 'nobody around here can beat you' talk that put me on a pedestal in the first place."

Rob leant in and kissed Faye on the forehead. She was thawing a little, but still unimpressed.

"Nothing to do with being eighteen stone and six foot six, then? Nothing to do with the broken cheekbones and the broken eye sockets from one bloody punch?"

"He came at me with a cricket bat. I've never hit anyone first. Not ever."

"Stop trying to justify it."

"It's true."

"I don't like Liam hearing people talk about the things that happen in this town. Especially when the people telling the stories look up to you like you're a hero. It's a reputation built on violence."

"I haven't built anything. I've stuck up for my mates and I've defended myself. It's the soap watchers who think *EastEnders* is reality, they've talked me up."

"When Liam goes to big school, he'll have to live up to your reputation," Faye said. "The same way you had to live up to your dad's."

"He'd have to learn to look after himself anyway. It's part of being a man."

"I wonder if Jamie can say the same thing to Carl with a straight face."

"That's for Jamie to sort out. All I care about is providing for you and Liam. If I have to protect my friend from a beating now and then, so be it."

"What if you hit someone one day and they don't get back up? Have you ever thought about that?"

"Every time I connect, they go down. But would you rather they didn't go down and they got to me instead?"

Faye paused for a moment while she gave that one a little bit of extra thought.

"You could use Jamie as a shield?" she said.

Rob started to laugh.

"At last, some levity," he said, and pulled Faye into his chest. She let out a sigh, and Rob squeezed her until she fought to break loose.

"You know I'm right," she said.

"I love it when you're angry. 'The Incredible Sulk'."

Faye went to the mirror to sort her hair out.

"I like your rock chick look," said Rob.

Faye finished tidying her hair and looked at Rob in the mirror.

"You're still not off the hook."

Rob chuckled, then turned to Liam, who was back and holding a huge bowl of cereal.

"Mum, can we have fishcakes and chips tonight, please?"

"Thinking about tea whilst you're having your breakfast? I think you might take after me after all," Rob laughed.

"No chance," Faye chimed in. "But yes, sweetheart, you can have fishcakes, as you said please and are extremely handsome."

Liam was now too busy tucking into his breakfast and engrossed by *Ben 10* to care about soppy compliments from his mum.

"Uh-huh."

"I can get us a Chinese on the way home later if you like, Faye?" Rob asked, blatantly trying to get back in Faye's good books. This brought Liam's attention away from the TV.

"I can stay awake if you want!" he said, excitedly.

"Err, no. You'll be having fishcake and chips and then you'll be going to bed at a reasonable hour, young man," Faye said, causing Liam's shoulders to slump and his eyebrows to furrow.

"Do you not fancy some crispy duck, mate?" Rob said, smiling.

The disapproving look came back to Faye's face in an instant.

"That's not funny," she deadpanned.

"What?" Rob asked, turning to a grinning Liam and winking.

"You're not funny, and bringing up ducks after Carl nearly took out a swan with a stone is not big nor clever."

"Maybe they have Peking swan at The Golden Fleece. I'll check on the way home," Rob said, cowering when Faye marched towards him with a rolled-up newspaper.

"Stop it now. It's disgusting!" she said.

"Carl told me the sweet and sour sauce they have is cat blood," Liam said.

Faye's eyes were like daggers, and they were aimed directly at Rob, who gave her the 'oops' grimace and an expression that said 'It's all yours!'

"That's just stupid talk," she said.

"What is it made with then?" Liam asked.

"Umm, I don't know. Your dad can ask them while he's down there later."

"It'll be my pleasure, sir," Rob asked, taking a bow.

Liam finished his cereal and leant forward to put his empty bowl on the coffee table in front of him. Rob put paid to his laziness before he had the chance to put it down.

"Oh no you don't. Put it in the kitchen and then it's time to wash your bits, buddy."

Liam closed his eyes and sighed.

"Shift it," Rob said, and pushed him out of his seat. Liam stomped to the kitchen like he was wearing lead shoes.

"I don't *have* to have a bath, do I?" he said, starting the negotiations.

"Yes, you do. You stink."

"So do you," Liam said.

"I know. That's why I'll be having one after you."

"You can use my Homer Simpson bath foam if you let me go without one."

Faye put her hand to her mouth to hide her smile from the negotiator.

"I do like that stuff actually. Let me think about it," Rob stroked his chin as he pretended to give Liam's terms some thought.

"And?" Liam asked.

"And if you're not upstairs in ten seconds I'm going to kick you up the backside!"

Rob launched himself at Liam and growled as he chased the poor kid up the stairs. It was the fastest anybody in the house had moved in a long time, and Liam's combination of nervous laughter and screaming amused Rob greatly.

"That always works," Rob said on his return.

"You're happy that you terrify our son to the point that he squeals like a girl?"

"Yup."

Rob approached Faye from behind and put his huge arms around her. He kissed her neck, and she rested her head back and closed her eyes.

"Love you," he said.

"You'd better," she replied.

"I do. You know I do."

"Make sure you don't get too drunk tonight. You know he doesn't go to sleep properly until you're home. I don't like it when he sees you drunk."

"All I do is smile more and fall asleep on the sofa."

"Julie told me what happens when Jamie comes home drunk."

Rob broke away from Faye and rolled his eyes.

"You keep talking about Jamie like we're the same person!" he said.

"Julie said that Jamie burst into Carl's room instead of their bedroom whilst Carl was having a sleepover. He got completely naked and then collapsed on the floor," Faye said, deadly serious. Rob burst into laughter.

"I'll have him for this tonight!"

"You can't! Julie told me not to tell you."

"You failed."

"It doesn't end there. Jamie fell stark-bollock naked onto the four kids in sleeping bags that were camping on the floor. The kids ran out screaming, whilst Jamie laid there snoring so hard he almost swallowed a sleeping bag."

"I bet Julie went mental!" Rob said, still laughing hard.

"I think two of the kids are having therapy. Nightmares at the very least. It took a lot of free consultations for double glazing to keep the parents from pressing charges."

"I'm going to wind him up something chronic. I'll have him so paranoid he'll have to confess."

Rob was rubbing his hands together at the prospect of winding his friend up. Jamie was the master of the piss-take, as long as the ball never fell into his court. When that happened, he'd spit his dummy out and vacate the room as fast as possible. With this newfound evidence, Rob was going to have ammunition for a long time.

"Don't be getting Julie or me involved," Faye pleaded.

"Don't worry, I won't say anything. You're both safe."

"Good."

"Dad! I'm ready!" Liam shouted from the top of the stairs.

"Your number one fan is waiting for you," Faye said.

They shared a smile, then Rob went to the bottom of the stairs. He looked up to see Liam standing there, as naked as the day he was born.

"Put your sparrow away, buddy," Rob said, shielding his eyes.

"I want you to do the bath for me," Liam said.

"You're nine years old now, you can fill your own bath up."

"But I like it when you do it. You get the temperature right. I always burn myself."

Liam's voice was getting more and more whingey, and spurred on by the memory of Jamie's annoying son Carl, Rob gave in and Liam punched the air in victory.

"You're a devious little bugger. Put your winky away and I'll do it."

Liam laughed and covered himself up with a towel, and Rob followed him into the bathroom to work his magic on the blue and red taps.

Liam conducted the temperature test when the bath was filled. This started with the dunking of toes, then moved on to the shins, the goolies, and last but not least, the stomach and back. Once everything had been dipped and the shock had worn off, Liam could sit in a bath until he resembled a prune.

Liam laid down in the bath like a man without a care in the world.

"For a guy who didn't want a bath, you look very happy," Rob said.

"I am," Liam said.

Rob grabbed a measuring jug from the edge of the bath, dunked it in the water and then poured it over Liam's head. Liam closed his eyes and blew the excess water out of his nose, and Rob put the jug back on the side.

"Have fun," Rob said, leaving the bathroom.

On returning to the living room, Faye was polishing the coffee and dining tables. Rob interrupted her workflow by grabbing her and giving her a passionate kiss.

"What was that for?" she asked.

"Just wanted to," Rob replied, and kissed her again.

"Fair enough."

"Liam told me an amazing story about a koala bear today," he said.

"That's sweet, although I did tell him that they're not bears."

"Actually, I think I cocked that one up. He just said koala."

"Either way, that's sweet."

"It was, but I want you to be more careful with what you allow him to read from Mum from now on," Rob said, his mood turning more serious.

"What do you mean?" Faye said, frowning.

"The corpses of seven koalas in the road. Ring any bells?"

"I didn't see that bit. I'll make sure I read it over next time before showing it to him," Faye said.

"Good. I don't want him reading something like 'and then Roy got a redback spider bite on his nut sack' or something. He'll never sleep again. I've had to scrape enough corpses of spiders off his Penguin books as it is, and he's only been sleeping with the light off for a year."

Faye rolled her eyes.

"OK, OK. You've made your point. I guess you're going to tell me now that what Jamie says in front of him is no worse than your mother's emails."

Rob smirked as he made that very realisation, albeit after Faye had mentioned it.

"Oh my word! You're right!" he said, milking the drama to the limit. "The moral high ground seems to have disappeared. Where is it?"

"Here," Faye said, sticking her middle finger up at Rob, right against his nose. She ignored his jibes and plugged the hoover back in. She finished off her cleaning, avoiding eye contact with Rob at all costs until the work was done.

Rob stood in the middle of the room like a dumb animal, desperately trying to make Faye laugh by pulling faces and doing stupid dances. When he realised he was not only going to fail at getting a rise out of Faye, but she wasn't even going to look at him, he went into the kitchen to munch on some cereal before it was time for his own bath.

3

Oatvale's town centre consisted of one main road, a market place and a large roundabout that took people to the edge of town or out into the country. Despite it being less than half a mile long, there were seven pubs scattered on its backstreets.

The worst pub was The Goat, which was notorious for fighting, drug use and underage drinking. The owner was Mark Harris, a forty-five year old stoner who had inherited a lot of money from his grandparents and bought his favourite pub on a whim, just so his mates had somewhere to drink. The Goat was renowned for its lock-ins, and you didn't want to be around when the patrons poured out into the streets at 5am. Projectile vomiting, punch-ups and backstreet sex were regular occurrences, and the poor neighbours could do nothing about it bar ringing the police or watching in disgust via their windows as drunks swayed down the street singing 'Tubthumping' at the top of their lungs, in between vomiting and pissing up the door of a Ford Escort.

The exterior of the pub was just as unwelcoming as its reputation. The windows were all but blacked out, the sign above the pub had been vandalised, and poor speakers blared out Britpop all day. Not the ideal place for a first date or a family meal, unless you lived on out-of-date pork scratchings.

The rest of the pubs were generally 'old men pubs', uneventful establishments that concentrated on keeping everyone over the age of fifty-five in ale and away from their wives. The exception to the rule was The Black Bull, which was owned by Charlie and Gail Winters, an Edinburgh couple in their late forties who had moved to the town in the early nineties and settled down after the birth of their daughter, Katie. The pub served homemade meals and had a long wine list, and Charlie was building an extensive collection of drinks that originated from places nobody in Oatvale could pronounce, let alone point to on a map. Charlie wanted to teach the town about the good stuff, and his beer menu featured over one hundred lagers, beers and stouts at present. It was his pride and joy, and it was arguably what was keeping the pub going. Sadly, at least seventy percent of the drinkers in Oatvale just wanted to go out and get annihilated on pocket change, rather than take out a second mortgage so they could pay £6 for a Scandinavian beer.

    Charlie opened The Bull at 11am every morning, and 'Weird' Tony Howard would be waiting outside in his tracksuit bottoms, 1994 Liverpool shirt and tweed jacket.

Tony was fifty-three years old and suffered from a number of undiagnosed mental illnesses, but the town had got used to him, and christened him 'Weird' Tony because they saw it as less hassle than trying to get him help. A stick-thin man with bulbous eyes, a handlebar moustache and a head of grey, curly hair, Tony resembled an ageing Leo Sayer – if he'd been struck by lightning.

"Orange juice, Charlie," he would say at 11:01 every morning.

"One orange juice coming right up," Charlie would say, pouring Tony a pint of lager instead.

This was a game that they had played every morning for the past five years, and it always made Tony chuckle. Tony would then empty the contents of his pockets on the bar, which consisted of about a tenner in pennies, screwed up receipts and fluff from his tracksuit bottoms. Charlie would take a few coins from the pile, but always less than the required amount. He figured that the longer he kept Tony in the pub, the less trouble he'd get into elsewhere. Tony would drink a few pints over the course of the night, before going home at around 10pm with a bag of chips from Frank's Plaice at the end of the road.

The Bull was a small, intimate haunt, and Charlie had spent a lot of money on making it feel like the cosy living room of a kindly grandparent. He had kitted it out with large comfy sofas and chairs, oak tables and stools, and installed a large wooden fireplace in the middle of the pub. This was a shrewd purchase that paid off in the winter, as the residents would become tranquil and docile due to the toasty atmosphere. The ones who didn't like it would leave for The Goat, leaving the appreciative beer drinkers behind.

As Tony enjoyed his first beer, Charlie lit the fireplace, throwing on some logs and stoking it until the flames rose. Tony would sit and stare at the flames, sometimes for thirty minutes straight, and the pub's regulars would place bets on how long each staring session would last.

Incredibly, and somewhat tragically, Tony had managed to father four children aged between eleven and eighteen, and all of them were familiar throughout the town for being violent, light-fingered, or with learning difficulties. People would often see them lurking around the streets at night with dirty faces and even dirtier clothes. But there was nothing they could do except call social services, or moan about it to their friends and family.

At midday on a Saturday, two bricklayers, Andy Bates and Ben Porter, would come to the pub to try a couple of Charlie's worldly beers, and end up staying until closing time. Charlie had known Andy and Ben since they were nippers and enjoyed their company, despite the fact that they were often rude and swore too much for his liking. Charlie used to host a post-match buffet for the local kids' football team, and their parents would have a few beers whilst the kids munched on vol-au-vents, sausage rolls and egg sandwiches. Andy and Ben were no longer kicking a ball around on a Saturday, but they had always enjoyed coming to the pub, and now they came for the ale instead of a handful of pickled onions and cheese cubes on sticks.

They were in their mid-twenties now, and had spent so much time together that they had started to look alike. The bricklaying had kept them in reasonable shape, and they were far from ugly, with cheeky smiles and baby-smooth faces. Andy had short, spiky brown hair and often sat with his mouth slightly open when he was lost in thought, which prompted Ben to roll up little pieces of paper and try to throw them into his mouth. When this worked, Ben would get a dead arm for his troubles, but it would be worth it to show Andy what a dope he was. Ben had lighter hair that was permanently slicked back like one of the wide boys from Essex, and his darker skin tone had led Andy to suspect that his friend was a secret sunbed user. He'd found no evidence as of yet.

People often assumed they were brothers, and Charlie liked to say that they were so joined at the hip he was convinced they were conjoined twins. They had grown up together through primary and secondary school, and when Andy's dad Pete could see that further education wasn't in his son's future, he offered him an apprenticeship at his building company. Andy's reply? Only if you take Ben on too. He obliged.

The two friends were inseparable, yet they always fought, especially after a few beers. Fortunately, neither of them knew how to fight, and their handbags-at-dawn shenanigans soon died down and they were friends again within a couple of minutes. It was amusing to watch at times, and Charlie had the honour of observing them every Saturday.

"Gents," Charlie greeted them, as they plonked themselves down on bar stools next to Tony's mountain of change.

"How-do, Charlie?" Ben said, pulling himself up onto his seat.

"I'm good, gents. Been busy this week?"

"As a prostitute-for-a-pound sale in Soho, Charles. You?"

"Aye. Tony's a walking wallet," Charlie said, sarcastically. "He wipes his nose with a twenty pound note and his arse with a fifty."

Ben chuckled. He took off his smart black jacket and placed it on the empty coatrack at the end of the bar. He was the more smartly dressed of the two, with a fondness for a jeans-and-jumper combo. He would always wear the jumpers that had the tops of shirts sewn into them, as he felt they made him look 'smart-casual'. Andy was more of a 'chav chic' kind of guy. He'd buy an armful of flannel shirts and Lee Cooper jeans from Sports Direct and live in them year round. The *Brokeback Mountain* jokes tailed off after a few months.

Charlie joyfully pushed a black folder in front of his two customers.

"We don't want to see your gay porn portfolio, Charlie," Andy joked.

"Cheeky little shit," Charlie fired back. "This is my masterpiece. And it's nearing its conclusion."

Andy flipped the folder back to reveal Charlie's beer menu. At this point, it was A4 paper in plastic pockets, but it was taking shape nicely. The menu was divided into sections based on location, and Charlie grinned in anticipation as Andy and Ben looked through the pages.

"What d'ya think?" Charlie asked.

"Looks good, Charlie," Andy said, nodding like a dog.

"Can't pronounce a single one of 'em, like. But that's probably a good sign," Ben said.

"Look at the Belgian section. Charlevoix Dominus Vobiscum Lupulus. Strong ale. Ten percent," Charlie said, smiling like a proud parent showing baby pictures to his friends for the first time.

"Bastard," Andy said, in a hushed whisper. "You'd be on your arse after three of them."

"Probably tastes nice, too."

Charlie shook his head, but was pleased that the two of them were at least taking an interest in his passion project.

"What can I get you, lads?" he said.

"Two pints of Fosters, please."

"Are ya kidding me?" Charlie said, his proud smile evaporating and being replaced by a frown. "I show you my list and you order Fosters?"

"It's noon, Charlie. We'll get to your fancy beers, don't you worry."

Charlie poured the two pints whilst muttering his disapproval. He placed the beers in front of them and took the money from a wad of notes that Andy and Ben had put on the bar. Ben had started doing this ever since he'd seen the Aussies doing it in a film he had watched, and liked that he didn't have to keep delving into his wallet to pay for every drink. He and Andy would put their money together, place it on the bar, and when it ran out, so would they. A good plan.

Andy and Ben simultaneously sipped on their ice cold pints, before smacking their lips and saying 'ahh' in an expression of pleasure.

"There's nothing better than the first swig of your pint after a tough week at work," said Andy.

Tony had been staring into the fire for twenty minutes, and had now finished his first pint. He placed his empty glass on the bar, and Charlie filled it back up. Tony only ever drank from the same glass, as he was convinced that the government were trying to poison him. When asked why the powers that be would target him, Tony simply replied: "I know stuff." That was good enough for most people.

Charlie threw together some of Tony's change and chucked it into the till, and Tony stood close enough to Ben that he felt like he had to acknowledge his presence.

"Alright, Tony?" Ben asked.

No answer. Tony went back to the fire.

"I wonder what he can see that we can't," said Andy.

"I don't think he's that complicated," Charlie said, and loaded last night's empties into the glass washer by his feet.

"He's certainly a character," Ben said, glancing over his shoulder at him.

"D'ya hear that, Tony?" Charlie called over. "These two think you're a character."

No response.

"That fire must be fucking interesting if he's going to stare at it all day," Andy said.

"Why are you so interested in what Tony's up to?" Ben asked.

"Because he's standing right behind me, and he's as crazy as a shithouse rat, that's why. He doesn't exactly fill me head with comforting feelings."

"Fair dues," Ben said.

Charlie's cleaning rota was stuck to the shelves at the back of the bar with Blu-Tack, next to the five hanging optics for house vodka, gin, whisky and dark and white rum, and behind the special malt whiskies from his native land, which nobody drank except for him and his wife at the end of a busy shift. There was nothing quite like a sup of Talisker after you'd just kicked a bunch of degenerates out into the street. Charlie was a regimented cleaner, and would often state that 'cleanliness is close to godliness'. Gail figured that her husband had OCD, and the amount of the invoices for D10 cleaning spray would support her theory. Still, it kept him busy when times were quiet.

"I suppose more people will come in later, Charlie," said Ben, already getting bored.

"I certainly hope so," Charlie replied, spraying and scrubbing the bar surfaces.

"People aren't going out as much as they used to," Andy observed. "Tesco and Asda have both got good deals on booze."

Charlie put down his D10 and cloth and frowned at Andy.

"What's that supposed to mean?" he said.

Andy, sensing that he'd struck a nerve, sat upright in his chair.

"Nothing, Kim and Aggie. You go back to cleaning. I was merely making an observation."

"Well don't. I have six pubs to contend with, let alone the bloody supermarkets. I don't want to hear anything more about recessions, supermarkets or anything else that might be taking money out of my tills, ta very much."

Ben put his head down and tried to contain his laughter, but failed. He snorted into his lap.

"And you can stop behaving like a child as well," he continued.

Ben held his hands up to apologise.

"Sorry, Charlie," he said.

Charlie stopped in his tracks and held his stomach. He grimaced in pain for a moment, and waited for it to pass. The lads looked concerned.

"You alright there, Charlie?" Andy asked.

"I'm fine. I just…" He paused.

"What?" Ben asked.

"I haven't been able to pass for a while?" Charlie finished, a little embarrassed and expecting to be ridiculed by the two men at the bar.

"Don't worry about that, Arsenal have had that trouble for years," Ben joked.

"Cheeky bastard!" Andy said. He threw Tony's tracksuit pocket fluff at him for good measure, and Ben flapped like it was acid.

"Fuck off, you dick!" he cried.

Charlie rubbed his stomach as the pain passed, and concentrated on voicing his disgust at his customer's language instead.

"Oi! You can cut that swearing out or you can go somewhere else," he said.

"I'm sorry, Charlie," Andy said. "I couldn't help myself. What's really up with your guts there?"

"I can't go to the toilet," Charlie said.

"You can't shite?" Ben said, earning daggers from Charlie in response, and causing him to apologise instantly. "Sorry, I meant 'poo'."

"When was the last time you had a poo, Charlie?" asked Ben.

"I'm not going to talk about this with you two, like some twisted Sesame Street sketch."

Charlie backed away from the bar and picked up his D10. Then he grimaced again. Andy tutted.

"Maybe we can help you?" he said.

"Three days," Charlie blurted out.

"Three days you haven't pooped?" Andy replied.

"Yes."

"Why do you think that is?" Andy asked.

"Don't you think I've thought about that? It's not a bloody lifestyle choice," Charlie said, his voice growing more and more agitated.

"You're going to look like Vyvyan from *The Young Ones* soon, Charlie," Ben chimed in, helpfully. "Y'know when they think he's pregnant but it's just one big fart?"

Andy and Charlie ignored Ben, who shrugged it off and continued drinking his pint.

"D'ya think it's from stress?" Andy asked.

"I have a business that's hanging on by a thread and an eighteen year old daughter who wears skirts smaller than a flannel. I'd say that might qualify as reason to be stressed."

Andy decided to steer the conversation away from the subject as quickly as possible.

"Sorry, Charlie. We came here to escape the trials and tribulations of work and here we are taking a king-sized Snickers of a shite on your working day," he said.

"Your apology is accepted, although not needed. My wife tells me I worry too much," Charlie said, beginning to calm down and even managing to smile a little.

"If it makes you unable to poo, I would agree with her," Ben said, picking the worst moment to rejoin the conversation. "Where is Gail?"

"Shopping," said Charlie, taking deep breaths to get through his stomach pains.

"Shopping!" Andy shrieked. "Here you are, slaving over us and sitting in silence opposite scary Tony, blowing up like a hot air balloon over not-pooing stress, and Gail is off adding to the national debt."

Andy's theatrical response brought a smile to Charlie's face.

"Spending money is actually good for the economy, Andy. But thank you for your concern. Besides, she's only gone to Tesco," he said.

"Tesco, al fresco! You can buy plasma screen TVs at Tesco! I went in there with my Nan last week. Two hours later, I'd eaten a fried breakfast, bought two Jason Statham DVDs, and left – forgetting I'd left my Nan in there. I only went in for tea bags."

"She's just getting milk for the coffee machine," an amused Charlie said.

Ben shook his head and looked at Andy like he had escaped from somewhere.

"How have we been friends for this long?" he asked.

"What?"

Ben ignored his friend and finished his pint. He placed the empty pint glass at the edge of the bar in front of Charlie, then slammed his fists down on the beer menu folder.

"Right! We'll have two of those Belgian bastards please, Charlie. And we will have no more talk of poo, or lack thereof. Are we all agreed?"

Charlie nodded and cleared the empty glass. He opened the beer fridge and took out two bottles that resembled bottles of Babysham. Andy and Ben looked less than impressed, and they sneered as Charlie poured the beer into odd-shaped glasses that didn't look anything like their usual pint glasses.

Ben shook his head, as if to shake the image of the feminine beer glass from his mind, and motioned for Andy to neck the rest of his pint.

"Hurry up and drink that, Fanny Wet Legs," he said.

Andy duly obliged, finishing just under half a pint in three seconds.

A proud Charlie placed the drinks in front of the two men as if they were the Holy Grail, and took £20 from the pile of notes on the bar.

"A twenty?" Ben said, despairing. "I hope there's some change coming, Charlie."

"You're paying for taste in this establishment, lads. And I thank you."

"Your bank manager's thanking you, you constipated bastard," Ben muttered under his breath. Fortunately for him, Charlie didn't catch it. He was too busy reading the empty beer bottle, which cost more than Andy's shirt, jeans and shoes combined.

Andy and Ben toasted each other with their strange, rounded beer glasses, which had a stem at the bottom and resembled an overweight wine glass. They were clearly uncomfortable, but went ahead and tasted it anyway. Their frowns faded the second the ale touched their lips, and Charlie watched with a fat grin on his face as he awaited the verdict.

"What d'ya think?" he asked.

Andy placed the glass down on the bar and licked his lips.

"Headache juice," he said.

Undeterred, Charlie looked to Ben for a more cultured review of the beverage. Ben's glass touched the bar, and then he belched. It was loud enough for Tony to dip at the knees and spin around like he had just heard an air raid siren, before staring back into the fire again.

"Did I just scare Tony?" Ben asked, smiling, but too afraid to turn around.

"Yes you did, you fool," Charlie said, disappointed in him. "I knew I was wasting my time with this."

Charlie took the folder away from the bar, causing Andy and Ben to moan at the loss of their new favourite book, and the only one they could probably read through to the end without getting bored.

"I'm sorry, Charlie," Ben said. "I just had wind. It's a glorious drink, I promise. Glorious."

"Yeah?" Charlie asked, smiling.

"Fantastic."

"What do you think, Andy?" Charlie asked.

"I think it's going to be the cause of many a fight outside The Goat," he said, causing Charlie to shake his head in disagreement. "This is loopy juice, mate."

"People who drink this stuff aren't going to be traipsing over to that shithole afterwards. This is going to become *the* place to go to for a sophisticated night out. I'm going to lead the way for the other places to clean up their act."

Andy and Ben nodded along with Charlie's inspired pitch. Deep down though, they knew it would only be a matter of time until the demand for cheap beer would put an end to his pipedream, regardless of how sincere it was.

They knew that you could get away with sophisticated ideals in country pubs, where there was no choice, but in the town centre, where competition was rife, you were on a hiding to nothing.

"Wood burns," said Tony, before leaving the fireplace for the bathroom.

"Yes it does, Tony. Yes it does," Andy said, trying not to laugh.

"I can't believe you let him in here," Ben said, shaking his head at Charlie.

"What am I supposed to do with him? Kick him out? What would he do? Where would he go?" Charlie asked, whilst Ben nodded along and shrugged his shoulders to the questions he posed.

"You're not going to do well on the sophistication front with Weird Tony staring at the fire and wandering into the bogs every five minutes. Disappearing and reappearing like Houdini," Ben said.

"Who?" Andy asked.

"Dini."

The door of the pub swung open, and they could hear the strength of the wind outside. It was a cold and miserable day, so business would be slow until at least seven o'clock, which meant that Charlie's entire day would be spent with Tony, Andy and Ben. Good times.

Fortunately, the door had opened because Charlie's beloved wife Gail had arrived, and she traipsed through the bar carrying three Tesco bags, which made Andy raise an eyebrow and give Charlie a look that said: "Just milk?"

Charlie's face lit up when he saw her, and for good reason. Firstly, he loved her more than anything in the world, and secondly, he knew he was a lucky bastard. Gail was an attractive, confident woman, and you wouldn't want to mess with her. She was the disciplinarian of the pub, and not afraid to kick you into the street if you misbehaved.

"Hello, light of my life," Charlie said, leaning over the bar and giving her a kiss on the lips.

"I've bought a few things. Here's your milk," she said, placing it next to the coffee machine. She looked over to Andy and Ben, who were both grinning at her like schoolboys with a crush on their teacher.

"Hello, boys."

"Hi, Gail!" they said in unison, their voices pitched a little higher than usual.

Charlie shook his head at how wet the pair of them became around his wife, who had launched herself across the bar and grabbed one of the empty bottles of Charlevoix Dominus Vobiscum Lupulus.

"Wow, you guys are drinking the Charlevoix!" she said, excitedly.

"Yeah, yeah, we're sophisticated now," Andy said, winking at Ben.

"This stuff will blow your roof off if you're not careful. Don't have more than one, especially not at lunchtime, you maniacs."

"We'll be alright, Gail," Ben laughed.

"I've seen you throw up on yourself and walk home in it, Ben. Trust me, only have one of these."

Andy chuckled at Ben's expense, who shut up instantly.

"Wanna join us for a non-headache beverage, Gail?" he asked.

"No thank you, Andy. I've got to pick Katie up from yoga."

Ben perked up when he heard Katie's name mentioned, like a dog who hears the front gate open and the sound of footsteps up the garden path.

"How is Katie? Eighteen now, isn't she?"

Andy closed his eyes at Ben's stupidity at asking that kind of question. Gail's back straightened and her eyes zoomed in on Ben, like rockets honing in on a target.

"Yes, Ben. Are you planning a birthday party for her?" she asked, zero emotion in her voice.

Ben shook his head and his throat made a strange sound, born from fear and awkwardness. Gail knew as well as anybody that in a small town, any girl with an ounce of attractiveness was going to be set upon by the wolves. But she also knew that they'd have to get past her first.

Gail turned to Charlie, who was back on D10 duties.

"I'm going to put these away and then I'm off," she said.

"OK, sweetheart. See you in a bit."

Gail took the stairs in the back of the bar to the two-bedroom flat above the pub. Charlie and Gail had chosen not to buy a house in town, so they could save as much money as possible whilst living in the pub, before heading back to Scotland when they retired with a little pot of gold.

Andy sipped his beer and stared into the glass for a moment.

"I like this beer. It's a grower. I think I'm going to go to Belgium."

"I went to Belgium with the ex," Ben said.

"Did ya?"

"Yeah, I told you. We went to Brussels on a bus."

"Did you meet Van Damme?"

"Once," said Tony, returning from the toilet and taking pride of place in front of the fire again.

"Thanks, Tony," said Ben. "It was really expensive, but they had tons of beer like this one, and they all came in gay glasses, too. We took another bus to this other town, and there was horse shit everywhere. Loads of chocolate though."

"They should hire you as a tour guide," Charlie said, heating up the milk for his latte on the coffee machine.

"It was weird. Nobody seemed to pick up the horse-do. It made me wonder if they had pooper scoopers in Belgium."

"No wonder you're single. What a romantic conversation that must've made for."

"I didn't mention it to her, I just Googled who invented them when I went home."

"And?" Andy asked.

"Brooke Miller."

Silence.

"You're a fucking idiot," Andy said.

"Did he invent anything else?" Charlie asked, if only to stave off the boredom.

"Flame thrower," Tony uttered from beside the fireplace.

Andy shook his head and jumped down from the bar stool.

"That was a riveting story, but now I need to break the seal."

"Me too," Ben said.

They headed for the men's room together, and Charlie stood and watched them go. He looked over to Tony, who had been staring into the fire for three minutes straight. He wondered who was crazier: Tony, Andy, Ben or himself, for still running a pub in this town. Before he could answer his own question, the milk boiled over onto his hand and he screamed in pain.

4

Liam's bedroom was a Marvel fan's wet dream. There were three *Iron Man* posters adorning his walls (one for each film), and a gigantic *Avengers Assemble* poster above his bed. Waking up to see Captain America, Hulk and Thor staring back at you was a great way to start the day if you're a young boy, even if most of Liam's attention had been taken by Scarlett Johansson in recent weeks.

The walls of his room were painted in navy blue, and the room was kitted out with a desk and wardrobe, a TV, a DVD player and an Xbox 360. At the end of the bed there was a large brown bear, which Liam was given on his first birthday and had kept ever since. It was tatty as hell, but Liam said that was part of Freddy's charm.

Every night at 7pm, Liam would be sent upstairs to brush his teeth and get ready for bed. By around 7:30pm, he would be in bed and was allowed to watch thirty minutes of TV before lights out. Those thirty minutes were usually taken up with some kind of superhero series, although the Pixar box set got a lot of playtime too.

If he wasn't in the mood for TV, Liam would read one of the many books he had on the shelf above his bed. Faye had recently bought him a fifteen-book collection of Roald Dahl, and he was making his way through them. His personal favourite was *The Twits,* but *The Witches* terrified him, especially after watching the film version with Anjelica Huston as the Grand High Witch.

Rob went out on Saturday nights, and Faye would send him up to say goodnight before he left, otherwise Liam wouldn't be able to sleep. Liam always commented on how smart his dad looked, followed by a remark about his aftershave. Rob didn't make a huge effort when he went out, but when you're used to seeing your dad in overalls or a joggers-and-hoodie combo, the sight of him in jeans and a tucked-in shirt was like seeing a tramp in a tuxedo.

Rob knocked on his son's door three times, then popped his head around the door. Liam sat up and put the book he was reading to one side.

"Hey, buddy," Rob said, and sat at the end of his bed.

"Hiya," Liam said, smiling. "You look nice."

"Thanks," Rob said, looking down at his blue and black chequered shirt.

"That smells strong," Liam said, scrunching his nose up like a rabbit.

"Your mum buys me this every year for Christmas. I've still got five bottles of it left. I think you'd better start using it so we can get rid of it all."

"Umm, no thanks."

"You don't like it?" Rob laughed.

"It's OK. Why don't you just ask her to stop buying it for you?"

"Good question. I guess it makes her happy to buy it for me," he said, before noticing the book by his pillow. "What are you reading at the minute?"

"*The Mouse Butcher* by Dick King Smith," Liam replied, which made Rob's face light up. He reached over and grabbed it, and flicked through the worn copy like he had unearthed his childhood diary.

"I loved this book!" he said. "I was obsessed with it. My dad bought it from a jumble sale for me, and my mum used to read it to me all the time. This is that exact same copy, did you know that?"

"Yup," Liam nodded. "It's really old."

"Hey, less of the old," Rob said, and prodded Liam's chest, which made him laugh.

"I've been thinking," Liam said, sitting upright.

"Uh-oh, should I be worried?" Rob asked.

"No. I was wondering what Granddad was like? You and Mum never really talk about him. Why is that? I talk about you all the time to my friends."

Rob thought about this one for a moment. He knew that it was wrong to underestimate a child's ability to understand, yet at the same time he wasn't entirely sure he was willing to talk about it.

"I've not been asked that for a long time," he said.

There was a long pause.

"Do you miss him?" he asked.

"Every day, yeah. He was a big man, like me. He worked a lot, so we didn't get to see a lot of him. But he always made a point of coming into our rooms when he came home after a beer on a Friday night, and telling us a story."

"What kind of stories?" Liam asked, intrigued.

"Funny stories. Like the time he got drunk and fell asleep in an old lady's rose garden. In the morning she came out and set the dog on him, and he leapt over her fence and ran home. When he got in, he realised he'd slept with his face rested against a garden gnome, and he had a perfect gnome-face imprinted on his cheek. That took some explaining to your grandma."

Liam laughed.

"I don't understand why people drink. Beer smells disgusting," he said.

"It's a social thing. You go out, meet your friends."

"Then you get drunk?" Liam asked, still unconvinced.

"Sometimes. You don't have to though."

"I'm never going to get drunk," Liam said.

Famous last words, Rob thought.

"How come you never tell me any stories?" Liam asked.

"I just did," Rob said, attempting to dodge the question.

"Not Granddad stories, *your* stories."

Rob looked up at Scarlett Johansson as he searched his memory for a good story.

"I've got a good story about Granddad, from when I was your age. Wanna hear that one?"

"Yeah!" Liam said, excitedly.

"OK, here goes."

Liam prepared himself for story time by flattening his pillows and lying down.

"Your grandma never used to let me and David watch TV later than six o'clock, and we were sent to bed at seven every night."

"Like me?" Liam interrupted.

"Yep, like you. We're supposed to learn from our elders and pass it down to the next generation, you see."

"What are you going to pass down to me?" Liam asked.

"My good looks and this story, if you stop your jabbering!"

Liam laughed and lifted his bed cover so it hid his grinning mouth.

"Anyway, me and your uncle David were absolute horrors to get to sleep. We'd have pillow fights, we'd tell each other jokes – anything to stop from going to sleep. Mum came up with a plan to make us behave and go to sleep: she told us that if we weren't asleep by eight o'clock we would be in trouble, because all the dolls and toys and teddy bears came to life at night."

Liam's eyes grew to the size of dinner plates.

"We slept like babies from then on."

"That's terrifying," Liam whispered.

"Worked though," Rob said. "Anyway, there was one night where your grandma had the rare chance to go out on the town with her friends, and we were left with your granddad, whose babysitting skills weren't exactly great. He would just shout threats up the stairs and we'd hide under our blankets in silence until we fell asleep. This time would be the last time he was trusted to look after us."

"What happened?" Liam asked.

"We couldn't sleep, and as the clocks passed 8pm, we were so convinced that the teddies were going to come alive and get us, we thought, 'Let's go to Dad and he can stop them'. We could hear the sound of the TV, so we knew he was downstairs, and that we'd be safe if we could make it there without any of the teddies seeing us. We wrapped ourselves in our blankets like E.T., and wandered downstairs. We sneaked into the living room, and your granddad was snoring like a bear in his favourite chair. We climbed up on the sofa and watched him sleeping for a bit. It was really funny, because he was catching flies with his open mouth and his tongue kept moving from side to side as he snored."

"You do that sometimes," Liam said.

Rob laughed and shook his head to deny all knowledge.

"After we got bored of laughing at Granddad's snoring, we started watching the film that was playing on the TV. There was a young boy in his bed, not much older than us, and he looked worried. Then we saw it was an evil-looking clown sitting on the rocking chair at the end of his bed that was worrying him."

Liam's pupils dilated.

"It was a sinister-looking clown. The boy couldn't take any more of it staring at him, so he tried to throw a T-shirt over it. But he missed. Uncle David looked at me, and we wrapped ourselves up in our blankets even tighter. In the film, the boy had decided to turn around and try to go to sleep, but the clown was never going to be far from his thoughts."

"I have this when I've seen something scary on tele. Every time I close my eyes, I keep seeing it," Liam said, still fascinated by the story.

"Eventually, the boy managed to drift off. But soon enough, a bump made him wake up again. He looked up toward the end of his bed…"

Rob paused for dramatic effect.

"…And the clown was gone," he whispered.

Liam fidgeted in his bed.

"The rocking chair was slowly rocking, like something had just jumped from it," Rob said. "We sat trembling, convinced that your grandma was sending us a message to scare us back to bed. By the time we could work out what was going on, the evil clown jumped out from nowhere and attacked the boy."

Liam gasped.

"Uncle David and I screamed like a couple of choir girls. I mean, it could've shattered glass, it was so high-pitched. But instead of breaking glass it almost gave your granddad a heart attack, and he woke up with such a shock that he threw the beer can he was holding across the room on instinct. It hit the TV and it blew up."

Liam frowned and looked more than a little unconvinced by the last section of the story.

"It blew up?" he checked.

"Yep. The TV we had back then was the size of this room, and my dad had inherited it from his parents. It would've exploded if you'd added Channel 5 to it."

Liam giggled.

"So what happened next?"

"Your granddad had to buy a lot of flowers and chocolates to make it up to Grandma. Not to mention a new TV," Rob said.

"Did you ever find out what happened to the clown?" Liam asked.

"Oh, it was just some horror film that was on TV."

"It wasn't Grandma sending a message from a satellite or something?" Liam asked.

"Nope. I don't think she had access to satellites in those days."

"That's OK then. At least you could sleep that night, and it proved that the whole thing about dolls and teddy bears coming to life at night was made up."

"Yeah it did. It stopped me watching too much TV as well."

"Were you scared it was going to blow up?"

"Definitely, especially if my dad was around," Rob joked.

Rob soaked in all the childhood memories that the retelling of the story had brought back to him. He took the book from beside Liam and placed it back on the bookshelf above him.

"Time for sleep now, mister," he said.

Liam wriggled into sleeping position and gave his dad a loving smile.

"Thanks for telling me a story, Dad," he said. "You're not as good as Dick King Smith, but you made a solid effort."

Rob chuckled at his son's backhanded compliment, before playfully tickling him through his duvet.

"See you tomorrow, buddy."

"Love you," Liam said.

"Love you too, buddy."

Rob closed the door behind him as he left. The only light in the bedroom now was from the streetlight outside, which was shining through the tree in the front garden, and had found a gap in Liam's curtains. It was lighting the face of Freddy the teddy, and Liam was suddenly more wary of his old friend.

Liam took off his pyjama top and threw it over Freddy's head. He succeeded first time, and a contented Liam went to sleep, safe in the knowledge that Freddy's face was fully covered.

As Rob left Liam's bedroom, Faye was walking across the landing holding an ironing basket filled with Rob's work clothes.

"Were you eavesdropping?" Rob asked.

"No," Faye replied, clearly rumbled. "Is he asleep?"

"Not far off," he said.

Faye approached Rob and put the ironing basket by his feet. Before Rob could ask her what she was doing, she embraced him, and gave him a kiss on the cheek.

"That was really sweet of you," she whispered into his ear.

"What was?" Rob asked.

"It must've been hard for you," she said.

"Stop talking in circles." Suddenly it hit him. "Ah, so you were listening."

"I like listening to your little chats."

"I forgive you then," Rob said, and grabbed both of Faye's buttocks with his huge hands.

"Doesn't mean you get that," Faye said, pushing her bottom out to loosen his grip. She grabbed the ironing basket and walked to the end of the landing, before turning around and giving Rob a concerned look.

"Do you think you'll ever be able to tell him the truth about that night?" she asked.

Rob sighed and his posture slumped like he'd been punched in the gut.

"I don't need to talk to him about that stuff right now. All he needs to know is that I love him and that I'm always there for him. I'll see you later tonight."

Rob headed downstairs. Never one to shy away from a confrontation, Faye followed him into the living room.

"Don't you think it's better that he hears it from you?" she asked.

"He will hear it from me, when the time is right."

"The time is right now. You know it's only a matter of time before one of the kids in his class hears something and blurts it out to him. You remember what secondary school was like?"

Rob spun around to face Faye, who stopped dead in her tracks.

"What was that?" he asked, a deep frown on his face.

"What was what?"

"You flinched."

Faye shook her head and shrugged it off like it was nothing.

"No I didn't," she said, dismissively.

"Do you think I'd ever hurt you?"

Faye was riddled with guilt. She had pushed for a discussion that Rob was clearly hiding away from.

"I know you'd never hurt me. You just made me jump. It's not a big deal."

"It is a big deal when you're making me talk about shit I don't want to talk about. Yes, I know that Liam is going to learn stuff about this family that he won't like. And yes, I know that my father was a violent bastard and my school days were spent living up to his reputation. But what am I supposed to do about it?"

"Stay away from people like Jamie, and pubs like The Goat," Faye said, bluntly.

"And what? Just work my arse off all week and not allow myself an opportunity to let off some steam?"

"There are plenty of other places you can go to let off steam. Why don't you admit that there's a part of you that likes the reputation you have around here?"

"I like knowing that there's people around who respect me."

"And fear you," Faye said.

Rob stopped in his tracks.

"Crap rolls downhill, and your beautiful little boy, who wouldn't hurt a fly, is at the bottom of it. This is your opportunity to put an end to this small town bullshit once and for all."

Rob didn't say a word. He took his wallet and keys from the mantelpiece.

"I'm not trying to be a nagging bitch, I'm trying to protect our boy," Faye said.

Rob left the house. He knew that Faye was right, but he wasn't prepared to deprive himself of his weekly escape with friends. It was the male camaraderie at the end of the week that got him through the rest of it, regardless of how much he loved his wife and son, and as Rob approached the main street, he envisioned that first pint, and how good it was going to taste now that he was a little pissed off.

5

The kid was staring at Clive's headgear and trying to think what film it was where somebody was wearing something similar, and similarly horrific. A fat child of eleven years of age, his parents allowed him to do whatever he wanted, and as a result, he rarely ventured outside. His evenings and weekends were spent playing violent video games and watching anything with blood and guts in it on Sky Movies and Netflix.

All of a sudden, his eyes lit up.

Fight Club!

That's where it was from. The bartender with a birdcage for a head who thinks that Edward Norton is trying to test him when he asks who Tyler Durden is.

The euphoric rush of relief that flowed through the fat kid's body was more fulfilling than eating his body weight in chocolate, and he sat back in his train seat with a contented grin.

Ray and Clive had changed trains at Leicester after a ninety minute journey from London St Pancras, and they weren't impressed with their seating arrangement. Clive wanted to break the fat kid's nose for continuing to stare at him, and Ray was uncomfortable with having to look into the morbidly obese mother's eyes from across the table.

He wished that they'd sat opposite each other, but then he might have had to sit next to the fat cow.

Ray was a vain man, lean and mean looking with short cropped hair. He was thirty-five years of age but looked a lot younger due to a rigid moisturising and exercise routine. He was smartly dressed in a long cream-coloured moleskin coat, wore black trousers and polished brown shoes, and his patience was shorter than the collar of his Burberry shirt.

Before the headgear and car-crash-survivor face, Clive was a good-looking chap in his late-twenties. His black hair was gelled and combed back like a member of the Kray gang, and he was also dressed smartly in black trousers and a burgundy jumper. He was wearing a similar styled jacket, but in navy blue.

Clive took out a bottle of water and a box of higher-strength co-codamol, and threw five or six tablets into the water, turning it a strange shade of yellow. A mix of urine and Lucozade. He necked the water like it was his last drink on earth, which drew a disapproving look from Ray, and a horrified one from the fat kid's mother.

"How can you still feel your legs, let alone pain?" Ray asked, in a sharp South London accent.

Clive's eyes moved towards Ray, but he would have to move his entire body to turn and face him, and he wasn't going to waste energy doing that.

The lady opposite leant forward.

"You're going to damage your liver taking those things," she said.

"And you're the leading authority on health are you?" Ray fired back.

The lady sat back in her seat, offended and more than a little hurt.

"We should've drove. I hate trains," Ray said, looking out of the window at fields filled with sheep and cows, followed by the cottages and terraced houses of the small villages they passed. He fidgeted in his seat.

"You get tired when you drive," said Clive, before grimacing in pain.

"Why are you trying to talk?" Ray barked. "All you need to be able to do is point."

The train conductor announced over the tannoy that they were coming into the last stop before Oatvale, and the mother pushed her son out of his seat and gave the two men a dirty look as they left for the exit. Ray launched himself out of his seat and sat opposite his pained friend.

"That's better," he said, grinning. "I don't have to stare at the Toby Carvery All-Stars anymore."

Ray chuckled to himself. Clive closed his eyes and leant his head back into the headrest. Passengers came and went, and the train continued on its journey.

"Not long now, kiddo. Just hang in there a little longer. We'll have a couple of beers, find this prick, and everything will be rosy," Ray said.

"I don't think you're supposed to drink alcohol on these tablets," Clive said, drowsily, his eyes still closed.

"Well maybe you shouldn't be scoffing them down like fucking Smints, then."

"I would like to remind you that it wasn't long ago that I was on morphine, and my jaw and neck were smashed to pieces."

"I know, I know."

The friendly looking train conductor came by and checked tickets. A chubby grey-haired fella in his late-fifties, the conductor whistled as he worked, and stopped by Ray and Clive's table.

"Have I checked your tickets, gents?" he asked.

"You have, sir," Ray said.

"Okey dokey, right you are. I'd forget my head if it wasn't screwed on," he said, far too happy for a Saturday evening. "Where might you two gents be going?"

"We're getting off at the next stop," Ray said.

"Ah, lovely. It's a nice part of the world, this."

"Yeah?"

"Oh yes. Are you up to anything nice whilst you're here?"

"Just visiting a friend."

"That's nice. If you get the chance, get out to the surrounding villages and the countryside air. It'll make a difference to all the smog and traffic that you're used to down south."

"Sounds delightful," Ray said.

"It is. It is. Right, I'll leave you gents alone. Toodle-ooh."

"Toodle-ooh, mate."

Ray watched as the train conductor disappeared into the next carriage, before his smile dropped like a stone.

"Cunt."

Clive tutted, causing Ray to sit up straighter.

"What are you tutting at?" he asked.

"I don't like that word," Clive replied.

"That's because you can't say it."

"There's no need to be cruel."

"Sorry, mate. I'm just on edge, y'know?"

"I know. I would be too, if I could feel anything," Clive said, attempting a smile that quickly turned into a painful squint. "Have you thought about what you're going to say to him?"

"I don't know. I've been trying to come up with a cool one-liner, like Bruce Willis in *The Last Boy Scout* or something like that. Then there's a part of me that wants to get the full-on shit-your-pants moment of impact, which you can only get if it's a surprise. I keep going back and forth on the idea."

"What have you come up with? For the one-liners, I mean," Clive asked.

Ray paused for a moment, before delving into his coat pocket to pick out a four-way folded piece of paper.

"You wrote them down?" Clive said, and cracked another painful smile.

"Yeah, yeah. Don't break your face over it, smart-arse. D'ya wanna hear 'em or not?"

"Go for it. If I close my eyes, it's because of the painkillers. Not the painfully bad one-liners."

Ray allowed himself to laugh at that one. Touché, he thought. After all, Clive was the one with the broken face, not him.

"Here goes. Number one: 'Hey buddy, remember my friend? Now remember this... *Boosh!*'"

Ray imitated a gun going off, and Clive closed his eyes and snorted out of his nose.

"Was that a laugh or the sound of you dying?" Ray asked.

"A bit of both," Clive replied.

"Reserve judgement until you've heard them all, please."

Ray rolled his shoulders like he was getting into character to perform Shakespeare.

"Number two: 'You may think you own this town, but the only thing you own is the skid marks in your pants.'"

No reaction from Clive.

"Are you awake?" Ray asked.

"You asked me to reserve judgement until I'd heard them all."

"It's hard to gauge your reaction when you've got your eyes closed."

"Just keep going."

"OK. Number three: 'Your ass made my friend's face into grass, but I'm the lawnmower.'"

Silence.

"Number four: 'Greetings from London, cocksnogger.'"

Clive's cheeks expanded as he held in a belly laugh that would likely rupture his entire face.

"Ah, you like that one. Right, numero cinq: 'It's boom time, you townie bastard.'"

Ray folded his letter back up and put it back into his pocket. Clive opened one of his eyes, saw that Ray's pitch was over, and then opened the other one.

"What did you think?" Ray asked, and waited for Clive's approval.

"First of all, promise me you're not going to get angry," Clive said.

"Yeah, I promise," Ray replied. "Do it. Hit me with it. Go for it."

"OK. First of all, the one-liner idea doesn't really work. For a start, you read them from a piece of paper. Unless you memorise them quickly, you're not going to leave yourself a lot of time to go from holding and reading to pointing and shooting."

Ray stared forward, open-mouthed.

"Secondly, you want the one-liner to be short and direct. Your first one was like Coronation Street on smack. The others just didn't make sense. I liked the word 'cocksnogger' though. That was funny."

Ray continued to stare forward. For Clive, it felt like hours before his friend sat back in his chair and stared out of the window. The sky was now pitch black, and it had started to rain.

"We'll stop off for a beer in the first pub that doesn't smell like piss and wait for the rain to stop," Ray said, watching the rain slide down the window in front of his face. "Maybe ask one or two of the locals where this guy lives."

"I remember there was a dirty Chinese restaurant at the end of the road where we had our first meeting. Maybe if we find a pub near there?"

"D'ya think it's a regular thing for him to do, then?" Ray asked.

"What else are they going to do in a shithole like that other than get pissed and eat Chinese food on the way home?"

"Good point. I'm a little peckish myself."

The conductor came by again, whistling something that resembled nothing remotely musical. Ray called out to him as he passed.

"Excuse me, chap," he said, and the conductor stopped for him. "Oatvale. Do you know it well?"

"Yes, sir."

"Excellent. Where's the best place to get a beer here? And if there's a Chinese as well, that'll be smashing. We're starving."

"Of course. There's a few nice pubs, but the nicest one is probably The Boatman, or The Black Bull. There's an open fire in that one, and it's on the main road. Follow the main road out and you'll find The Golden Fleece, which is a decent enough Chinese restaurant."

"That's great, mate. Cheers," Ray said.

"You're welcome," the conductor replied, wandering off down the carriage whistling his own variety of music.

Clive nodded his head the best he could for someone with no mobility from the neck upwards.

"The Golden Fleece. That's the one," he said.

"Yeah?" Ray asked.

"Definitely. I remember the name because it makes no fucking sense for a Chinese to be named after a Greek myth."

Ray laughed.

"I like the sound of The Black Bull. I love a pub with an open fireplace," Ray said.

"Let's not get too comfortable though. Remember what we're here to do."

"You don't need to tell me. I'm the one carrying the shooter."

Ray glanced over to a long and lean sports bag that was sitting in the overheard compartment above their heads.

"Are you scared? Not even a little bit?" Clive asked.

"Nope. You?"

"A little. This guy…" He paused. "He's dangerous."

"Yeah?"

"He did this to my face with one punch, Ray. One punch. A guy like that, you don't give him the chance to take a breath. You strike when you have the chance."

"Don't worry, he won't get the drop on me," Ray said, as cocksure as you can get. "You can be as hard as God's dick, but when I get that bad boy out for a run: game over."

Ray pointed up to the bag in the overhead storage. Clive attempted to smile again, and Ray continued trying to reassure him that everything was going to go to plan.

"Being the hardest man in a small town means nothing when you're staring down the barrel of a gun."

Clive's eyes lit up and for the first time in weeks, with the exception of when the morphine kicked in, he smiled correctly.

"*That's* your one-liner," he said.

6

On a Saturday night, The Black Bull was the pub you visited before The Goat, or used as a calmer alternative. This suited Charlie and Gail just fine. It was pointless trying to compete with The Goat, because if they lowered their prices, The Black Bull would become the new Goat, and they would sooner starve. The police and the folks who wanted a quiet pint preferred to have the rougher clientele in a pub that was off the main street. If those drinkers ended up at The Black Bull, the entire town would suffer as a result.

Andy and Ben were now on their sixth pint, and were using the bathroom every five minutes. Tony had fallen asleep in front of the open fire, his face slowly cooking as he dreamed. Andy had taken a series of selfies with him on his phone and uploaded them to Facebook, much to Charlie's annoyance.

Ben was reading a newspaper at the bar, tutting and sighing as he read stories of immigration, hate crimes and celebrity Botox. This drove Andy crazy, and he would curse him into silence depending on how theatrically Ben reacted to a story. Whenever he found one that particularly annoyed him, he zoomed in to read it more closely, before shaking his head and lifting the page out of the paper to show Andy and Charlie.

"Have you seen this?" he asked.

"I read the paper at seven o'clock this morning," Charlie replied.

Ben turned to his friend, who was shaking his head.

"Have you seen this?" he asked Andy.

"No. I was going to read it after you," Andy replied, clearly irritated. "But you decided to dictate it to me like Jacka-fucking-nory."

"I can't help it if I'm politically engaged," he said, causing Andy to spit beer out of his nose with laughter.

Charlie looked over to the two intoxicated friends as he finished pouring pints for his customers. He gave them his 'quiet down' look, but they were too busy barking at each other to heed the warning.

"You've read one newspaper in your life, and you have to read it out loud because you're a spastic," Andy said. "And when you're not reading it out loud you're mouthing the words. Politically engaged my swollen arsehole."

Ben turned back to his newspaper. He muttered something along the lines of 'I'm ignoring you, I'm not going to bite' and carried on reading. Andy observed closely to see if his lips moved when he read.

Charlie finished serving the customers at the bar before wandering over to Andy and Ben, wearing a frown that shaped four lines into his forehead.

"Listen you two," he said, surprising Andy and Ben with his sudden appearance. "Start acting like adults or I'm going to ask you to leave."

Ben pointed to his newspaper with both hands, like a kid showing his parents that he couldn't have scribbled on the wall with crayons because he was busy reading in another room.

Andy just nodded.

"No problem, Charlie," he said.

Ben used his palm and arm like a bar stool for his head so he could read in comfort. Andy interpreted this as a strop.

"Have you gone mardy now you've been told off?" he asked.

"I'm trying to read here," Ben snapped back. "I get the piss taken out of me for mouthing the words and reading aloud. I get whinged at by Charlie for sticking up for myself. What's a man got to do to read a newspaper in peace?"

"Calm down," Andy said. "I was only messing with you. Tell me a story."

"Piss off."

"Don't be like that. Go on. Tell us a story."

Ben's eyes narrowed. He didn't know whether Andy was trying to wind him up or not, but he decided to go ahead and read one out. Truth be told, he was dying to tell someone in the pub about it. He pushed the paper towards Andy and prodded the story with his finger. Andy started to read it, and before long, he was shaking his head and tutting just like his friend.

"Charlie!" he called out. Charlie looked over, still frowning at them, and continued polishing wine glasses. Andy waved him over.

"I've already read it," Charlie said.

"There's no innocence anymore," Andy called out. It caught the attention of a smartly-dressed forty year old man standing at the bar.

"What's that?" he asked.

Andy needed no encouragement. He lifted the story out of the paper and held it up for him to see. The headline read: 'Three year old boy has smoking habit'.

"Bloody hell," the man at the bar said.

"I know. Disgusting," Andy said.

Ben was more than a little miffed. Andy had taken his newspaper and – in a horrendous act of hypocrisy – was doing exactly the same as him, and to anybody who would listen.

"It's a badge of honour if you're pushing a pram at fourteen these days," the man at the bar said. Andy nodded in agreement, and continued reading. The man at the bar joined some friends at a table, causing Andy to turn to Ben instead.

"It says here that his mum caught him: 'It looked like he had been smoking for years,' the mother said. He's three!"

Ben shook his head. Andy's voice raised as he read the story aloud.

"Smoking for years? Was he smoking in the womb?" Andy looked down at his privates and put on a woman's voice. "'Ooh, I think a smoke ring just came out me fanny.' Disgusting."

"What are you doing?" Ben asked, bluntly.

"What?"

"You. Acting like a tit. Reading the story out like you're on Live at the Apollo. Shut up and finish your pint, you whopper."

"I'm just being 'politically engaged'," Andy said, doing the bunny ears for the words 'politically engaged', just to get the maximum wind-up effect from Ben. "It's all the rage now. They're even letting people who can't read without moving their lips do it."

"I'm going to knock your front teeth out," Ben said.

"Ah, calm down. Come on, let's read this story. It's actually quite funny."

Andy pushed the story between the two of them and they continued reading it.

"People like that should be castrated," said Charlie, from the end of the bar.

"Kids who smoke? That's a bit harsh," Andy said.

"The parents, you tit," Charlie said. "They should have a test that you have to pass in order to qualify for parenthood. It's the only way to save civilisation from being overrun by idiots."

"Bloody hell, that's a bit George Orwell isn't it?" Ben said.

"Who's that?" Andy asked.

"Plays left back for Villa."

"Oh."

"I think we've passed the point where common sense can be trusted in people," Charlie said.

Andy gave Charlie a concerned look.

"That's a depressing thought, Charlie. Have you not had a shit yet?"

"Be quiet," he said.

Andy leant over to Ben and whispered in his ear. "That's a yes."

Ben sniggered, but was heavily into the news story.

"I bet he has a five year old brother who smokes crack," he said.

"Or a twin sister that hands crystal meth out at playschool like sweeties," Andy added.

"Horrendous," Charlie said.

"The world has gone mad," Andy said.

"I bet you don't oppose twenty-four hour drinking though, do you? We all have our vices."

"I wasn't campaigning for twenty-four hour drinking when I was three though, Charlie," Ben said.

"You probably would have. Given the opportunity."

Andy nodded along in agreement, which displeased his friend.

"Why are you nodding along like you're not the biggest pisshead I know?" Ben asked.

"Because I *am* the biggest pisshead you know, and I'm proud of it."

"Fair enough," Ben said, finishing his latest pint. "Two more, Charles."

Charlie poured two more pints of normal beer. He knew that there was no point selling them the good stuff now. They were too pissed. It would all taste the same. It was better to save it for punters who would appreciate it than waste it on two drunks who wouldn't. He took the cash from the bar and threw it into the till.

"People are in too much of a rush to grow up these days," Charlie said, deep in thought.

"I know, Charlie. You're right," Ben agreed.

"I looked at my final year school photo the other day. I think about twenty of the two hundred people on there had lost their virginity, and there were only two pregnancies," Andy said.

"That's because you'd been expelled," Ben said. "If you'd have still been there it would have just been you in the photo, 'cause all of the girls would refuse to come without police protection."

"Very funny."

"Actually, why have you got a year photo if you weren't at the school at that point?"

"Nostalgia."

"What d'ya mean, 'nostalgia'?"

"I like to look back from time to time."

"I bet you just wank to it, you weirdo."

Charlie slammed his hands down on the bar in front of Ben, causing him to flinch.

"Stop using language like that, the pair of youse," he growled.

Ben held his hands up like he'd been caught stealing sweets from the local shop.

"Apologies, Charlie. Apologies. No more language."

"No more language from me, either," said Andy.

Charlie gave them the evil eye as he left the pair to serve a happy couple in their thirties that had approached the bar, and were looking through the wine list. This gave Andy and Ben some time to discuss their theories without fear of reprisal from Charlie.

"In the twelve years since I left school I've seen the teenage pregnancy rate become the worst in Europe, and all the young girls now dress like tramps," Andy continued.

"The teenage pregnancy rate is going up because you hang around outside schools when you're drunk," Ben replied, testing Andy's patience.

"I'm going to ignore that comment, and continue making my point like a gentleman."

"You're no fun."

"Here's a good example of the point I started to make before you started trying to get a rise out of me: Katie."

Ben's face scrunched up like Tony had come over and tried to kiss him.

"What d'ya mean? What's Katie got to do with it?"

Andy glanced over to make sure Charlie couldn't hear his theory about his only daughter. He was merrily discussing red wines with the couple at the bar, and was well out of earshot.

"Katie's eighteen and fit, right?" he said.

"Obviously."

"She's been flirting around older men for a lot longer than that though. It's like I said, it's not like the old days."

"I don't see how it's any different," Ben said. "You've just read too many Daily Mail headlines. There were still young girls gallivanting around, hanging out with older guys and sleeping around. You just didn't know about it because we didn't have the internet and twenty-four news coverage."

"Hmm… You make an interesting point."

"I know."

"Alright, don't get cocky."

"You want to get cocky with Katie. That's why you brought it up."

"No I don't. Anyway shut up, you'll get me killed. Or worse. Barred."

"Yeah, and who would pour your beer and listen to your shite then?" Ben asked.

"There's always The Goat."

"You don't have the chin or the reflexes for The Goat."

Ben laughed at that jibe, almost certainly because he knew it to be true. Ben, like so many folks, only went anywhere near The Goat when they were drunk enough not to feel the punches that landed on them, or when they had run out of stories to tell each other and wanted to collect a few for nights such as these.

Tony appeared behind the two and put his arm between them to grab the newspaper. He flicked through the pages and pointed to another story.

"Nasty," Tony said, and placed an empty pint glass on the bar for Charlie to fill up once he'd finished schmoozing with the couple in order to upsell the most expensive Rioja.

Ben read the story out. "'A man was stabbed in the throat outside a nightclub in London, before being thrown into a skip. He was found by a glass collector three days later.'"

Andy looked up to the ceiling as he tried to work out the logistics of such an appalling event.

"That doesn't make any sense," he said. "That means that the rubbish wasn't picked up for over three days. That'll attract rats."

"I think the man being stabbed and thrown into a skip was what the paper wanted you to focus on, Andy."

"Uh-huh."

Charlie brought over a fresh pint for Tony, who took it with both hands and muttered something to himself as he went back to the fire.

"Nasty business, that," he said. "There was a fight outside the club here the other weekend. You two were away. The bouncer with the vibrating eye..."

"Tom."

"Aye. He hit this kid so hard with a right hook I thought he was going to travel back in time. He hit his head on the pavement and didn't get up for twenty minutes. Katie was walking past and saw the whole thing. Ambulance and everything."

"The pavements are hard around here," Ben observed.

Andy shook his head at his friend's ridiculous comment.

"What was Katie doing out that late, Charlie?" Andy asked.

"She was supposed to be staying at her friends, but she got bored and came home. I was furious."

Andy nodded along, trying to contain the huge smirk that was fighting to emerge. Whether Charlie was choosing to live in denial or was simply oblivious to the fact, there was no way that a girl like Katie just happened to be walking past a nightclub at 1am.

"Who was it who got chinned?" Ben asked.

"No idea. But the guy didn't do anything but smile at Tom," Charlie said, shaking his head in disgust.

"That's all the encouragement he needs, the wobbly-eyed wanker. I put a Polo in someone's drink as a gaff once and he chinned me."

Charlie took a step back in shock and confusion at Ben's confession.

"It was a bit stupid to be seen to be putting something in someone's drink, Ben. There's adverts for date rape drugs everywhere," he said.

"They don't have a fucking hole in the middle, do they?" Ben asked, the injustice and humiliation coming back to him. "Do they have 'Polo' written round them? No! Any excuse to chin someone. Tom's an animal. He ruined my favourite shirt and in my sleep I shit myself."

"That's a usual night out for you."

Charlie allowed himself to giggle, although he felt a little guilty for doing so. Andy spotted this and played up to it.

"I bet he was tossing and turning in his sleep, chanting: 'Mint with a hole! Mint with a hole!'" he continued.

"That's enough now," Charlie said, containing his smile and going back to his cleaning duties.

The door to the pub opened and Katie breezed in. She had spent a lot of time on her hair and make-up and looked a good three or four years older than her eighteen years. She was wearing a pair of tight-fitting jeans shorts with black leggings underneath, and a smart black jacket on top. Andy and Ben's eyes followed her like a pack of cheetahs watching a gazelle as she made her way to the other side of the bar.

"Hello sweetie, how are ya?" Charlie asked, beaming as Katie gave him a hug and a kiss on the cheek.

Gail appeared behind Andy and Ben, who were still gawping at Katie.

"Still here, boys?" she asked, and they leapt out of their skins.

"Jesus, Gail!" Andy said. "I'm already using the toilet every five minutes."

"What are you reading there?" she asked, peering over Ben's shoulder at the London murder mystery.

"Three year olds smoking, Gail," Ben said, and flipped the pages back to the story.

"Crazy. It's like that girl from *E.T.*," she said.

Ben and Andy zoned out.

"Bit before your time, was it? Yeah, she was doing all kinds of stuff by the time she was ten, eleven."

Ben lifted the story up.

"Three, Gail. Saying that, you did LSD with me when you were eleven," Ben said, causing Andy to burst into laughter as the memories of taking hallucinogenics as a child came flooding back.

"That was a great night!" he said. "You told me zombies had taken over the world, and we hid in trees whenever a car drove past."

"Zombies can drive cars!" Ben cried out, imitating himself as a drug-fuelled pre-teen.

"We actually said our last goodbyes at the door to my house, d'ya remember?"

"Yeah. We thought that if our parents were zombies too there was a good chance we'd be eaten. I think you cried."

"I definitely cried. There's no shame in crying when you're facing death."

"Even an imaginary one."

"Sometimes they're the worst ones."

It was moments like these that made Gail wish that she lived anywhere else in the world.

Katie hopped onto a bar stool and sipped on a bottle of Diet Coke through a straw. Andy and Ben turned to her straight away, and Gail – more than aware of what was going on – moved on to speak to Charlie. She knew her daughter had more sense than to get involved with those two numpties.

"What are you ballbags talking about?" Katie said.

"Hi, Katie," Ben said. Not the answer she was looking for.

"Three year olds smoking, and E.T. doing drugs," Andy said.

"Fascinating. What are you up to tonight?" she asked.

"Nothing much. Stay here probably. Kebab then home."

"What an exciting life you both lead," she said, sucking on her straw.

"What are you up to?" Andy asked.

"Going to a mate's house. Gonna watch a film and eat some popcorn."

Andy smirked, which caught Katie's attention.

"What?" she said, a huge smile forming either side of the straw she had in her mouth.

"You're so full of shit," Andy laughed.

Katie put a finger to her mouth and Andy took the hint. He looked over to Gail and Charlie, who were chatting amongst themselves, and moved closer to Katie.

"We think you're seeing an older guy," he said. Ben nodded along.

"Really?" Katie said, playfully. "You think I like older guys do you?"

"Yup," Ben contributed. "And the sweet and innocent act that's fooled your folks ain't fooling us. We know you're up to no good."

Katie soaked up the attention.

"No comment," she said, springing off her stool and heading to her parents. "As entertaining as you lot *aren't*, I've got to go and get ready. Sees you later, Moms and Pops."

Katie gave her parents a kiss.

"Where are you off tonight then?" Andy called out, a smug look on his face as he knew the answer was going to be bullshit.

"I've got a seventeenth birthday party to go to. Gotta get into something more comfortable. See ya!"

Katie skipped upstairs, giving Andy and Ben a very discreet middle finger as she left. They turned to each other and grinned. It was the first time a girl had spoken to them in weeks, even if she was too much trouble for either of them. Charlie was soft as shit, but he'd kill for his daughter, and when he noticed Andy and Ben ogling her, he gave them daggers until they spotted him and pretended to be looking anywhere else.

Ben flicked the rim of his empty pint glass to break the mood.

"Keep 'em coming, Charlie," he said.

Charlie grabbed two pint glasses and started pouring, but his eyes never left Ben for a second. Ben could feel them burning into his skull.

"I'll keep more than drinks coming your way if you look at her like that again, you bastard," Charlie growled to himself.

People were vacating the pub in their droves. The food and wine punters would now head home, and the drinkers would head towards The Goat. From this point in the evening, all that remained were public schoolers who didn't fancy being punched in the face, and folks who appreciated sophisticated beverages in a warm, peaceful environment.

As a group of drinkers left, they were replaced by Ray and Clive, who strolled past Andy and Ben and stood at the bar. Ray was carrying the sports bag, and it scraped across the floor as he walked. The mood seemed to darken the moment they arrived, which was to be expected considering Ray's default facial expression was a frown, and he had perfected the art of chewing gum as a form of intimidation.

Ben was staring a little too closely at Clive's headgear, and Andy elbowed him discreetly so that he'd join him in staring down at the newspaper.

Charlie greeted the two men with a smile.

"Evening gents, what can I get you?" he asked.

"Two pints of Stella, please," Ray ordered, before sitting on a bar stool. His eyes scanned the room, and heads bowed as he made eye contact with anyone. He and Clive got settled, and Charlie placed two pints on the bar for them. "Are you gents hungry?" he asked.

"Nah, you're alright, champ," Ray replied. He took a swig from his pint and hummed his approval. "Tasty."

Charlie nodded his appreciation. He took pride in cleaning the beer lines twice a week to keep his tap beers clean and fresh, although when he told anyone this, they feigned interest. You had to be in the industry to care about these things.

Clive took a long black straw from the bar and put it into his pint. On any other day, and if it was anyone else in the world, Ben would've burst out laughing, but he was a little wary of the two men. He opted to use his peripheral vision whilst pretending to read instead.

"Are you from London?" Charlie asked, his voice going up at the end of the sentence as he made a fumbling attempt at small talk.

"How could you tell?" Ray said, not a fan of small talk either.

"Just visiting?" Charlie made a second attempt.

"Yes."

Charlie loosened up a little.

"Chaps from the nation's capital visiting our little town way up here. What brings you here, gents?" he asked.

Ray took another swig of his beer, and his eyes locked on Charlie. It seemed like an age before he answered, and it made Charlie pace with discomfort.

"Where in Scotland are you from?" Ray asked, ignoring the question.

"Edinburgh."

"What brings you all the way down here?"

Ray had a habit of sneering after everything he said, and at this point, Charlie decided that good customer service was not what these gentlemen were after. He took the money for the two beers and stepped back.

"I can see you're not the small talk type, fellas. I'll leave you to your bevvies."

Clive raised his glass to Charlie as he backed away.

Ben leant in to Andy and nudged him so that he wouldn't have to raise his voice.

"What's up with you?" Andy asked.

"Remember a few weeks back, when I told you about Rob having that fight?"

"The somersault?"

"I'm pretty sure it was a back flip," Ben said, still unable to agree with his friend for more than five seconds.

Gail entered the bar from the kitchen and slapped Charlie on the backside as she approached Andy and Ben.

"What are you two whispering about?" she asked. "I've had to cover our bloody kitchen porter again, so I need to hear some gossip."

"Stand in front of us so those two men can't see or hear us," Ben whispered, and Gail obliged. "I was walking back from The Goat the other week, and I stopped off at The Golden Fleece."

"The one that got closed down for using cats for their chicken balls?" Andy butted in, causing Ben to frown at him.

"That was a rumour... and if it tastes good, fuck it, why not... Where was I?"

"Golden Fleece," Gail sighed.

"Oh yeah. I stopped off at The Fleece for some grub, and Rob was in there."

"Rob Thomas?" Gail asked.

"Yeah. We were chatting a bit, and our food came out at the same time, so ended up wandering up the road together. We got up to Coombs Road, and there was a guy leant up against a lamp post. I said 'hello', just to be friendly like, and the twat starts mouthing off at us."

"Was he a cat activist?" Andy asked.

"No. It was the guy in the Terminator mask sitting at the bar right now."

"Fuck off," said Andy, dismissing his friend.

"What happened?" Gail asked, intrigued.

"He went nose to nose with both of us, asking us for a fag and invading our personal space. It was weird. Neither of us smoke so we said we don't smoke. So this Southern guy starts talking about how he's come up here and now he knows why he lives down there..."

"You really do have a way with words," a frustrated Andy butted in again.

"What?"

"Tell the story, you jabbering prick!"

"Am I not trying? Cock," Ben stopped to work out where he was in the story. "Anyway, after the guy stops slagging off where we live, he kicks Rob's sweet and sour chicken balls clean out of his hand."

Gail made a sound like somebody had scalded her. She knew that this story wasn't going to end well.

"Rob was not amused," Ben continued. "He landed one clean punch on the guy's chin, and he flipped in the air and landed on his face. Knocked. The. Fuck. Out. Funniest and most shocking thing I've ever seen."

"I've never understood why people start on Rob. The guy's a mountain. It's never going to end well for you," Gail said.

Andy's face was one of a man who was trying to work out one of life's great mysteries.

"I'm still pretty sure that's a somersault," he stated.

"Nope," Ben said. "A somersault is an acrobatic feat in which a person rotates around the somersault axis, moving the feet over the head. The somersault can be performed forwards, backwards, or sideways."

Andy and Gail looked at each other in utter bemusement.

"A back flip is a generic term for an acrobatic sequence of body movements in which a person leaps into the air, performs one complete backwards revolution while still in the air, and then lands on the feet."

"You've Googled yourself stupid," Andy said, laughing at his friend.

"If the man was launched by a punch, I don't think it's a back flip because it wasn't performed. And he didn't land on his feet. But then again it's not really a somersault either, because it wasn't an acrobatic feat, for the same reason." Gail was tying herself into knots as she allowed herself to be drawn into the debate.

"He went all the way round," Ben said.

Andy became animated as he came to his own conclusion about what had happened.

"Rob's punch has invented a new acrobatic feat: the somerflip! Hey, we should patent this," he said.

"Patent?" Ben said, confused.

"You know lots about acrobatic feats and Google, but sod all about the real world. You probably dreamt it, you twat."

"If Rob was here you could ask him. Why don't you ask *him*?" Ben nodded towards Clive. Andy put his head in his hands.

"Oh yeah, that's a great idea," he said. "'Excuse me mate, can you remember being somerflipped by a big guy for kicking sweet and sour chicken out of his hand?'"

"Very funny."

"What happened after the punch?" Gail asked.

"Rob made do with his Wong Tong soup and fucked off," Ben said.

Andy burst into laughter and leapt off his stool to go to the toilet. He passed a sleeping Tony, who looked like the dead mother at the end of *Psycho* as he sat open-mouthed in front of the fire.

"He's broken the seal," said Ben.

"That's lovely," Gail said, deciding that now was a good time to leave the two gossips to their own company.

Charlie took Gail's place in front of Ben, and he didn't look pleased.

"If only you two behaved like seals," he said. "I could throw you a ball and you'd shut up for hours. I don't want any trouble here, so keep your voices down and the topics of your conversation a little lighter. Please."

Ben grinned like a naughty child, which meant that any promise he made would be forgotten and broken in no time at all, especially when Andy returned from the toilet.

"No problem, Charles. Just keep pouring the beer and throw me a fish whenever I do a trick and we'll all be friends."

Charlie pointed at Ben, his standard sign language for 'behave!' The two Londoners were staring forward and finishing up their beers, and the lack of conversation or interaction between them was making the evening unbearably uncomfortable for Charlie.

Gail put a reassuring hand on her husband's back as she passed him and started making herself an espresso.

"Do you want a coffee, sweetheart?" she asked.

"I'm toying with the idea of a whisky."

"Whisky gives you heartburn."

"If I drink the whole bottle I won't notice it."

Gail smiled sadly at her husband as the coffee poured.

7

Every Saturday night, after Rob had left for a few pints with Jamie and his friends, Faye would pace around the living room. She imagined a nightmare near-future, where Rob started going out just to get away from her. It was common knowledge that Rob's best friend Jamie was out every Friday and Saturday just to get away from his wife Julie, and the pair were at each other's throats constantly. Whenever Julie came round for coffee and ranted about Jamie, Faye would stare at Julie's mouth and disappear into her own little world, before snapping herself out of it and thinking: "Do I ever sound like that?"

Faye made herself a big mug of coffee and sat down on the sofa with her laptop. She put her feet up on the coffee table – something she only did when Rob wasn't around, as he had an intense dislike of feet – and started up a Skype call with Rob's mother, Maggie.

Maggie's tanned and smiling face came up on the screen within a few seconds, and Faye brightened up immediately.

"Greetings from Brisbane," Maggie said, enthusiastically. A thin, attractive lady, Maggie used to dye her hair when she lived in the UK. Since living in Oz, she had embraced her grey, and she resembled an old hippy now, like the sort you see on TV shows about Byron Bay or documentaries on Woodstock. The look suited her though.

"Hi Maggie, how are you?" Faye asked.

"I'm good, I'm good."

"How's Roy?"

"He's alright, bless him. He's gone fishing with a few mates. Where's my boy?" Maggie asked.

"He's out on the town with Jamie," Faye said, the disappointment showing in her voice.

"Not the big one, the little one," Maggie laughed.

"Oh, he's asleep," Faye replied.

"I'll never get used to this time difference. We've only just woken up!"

Maggie was the kind of person who laughed at the end of almost every sentence, but it wasn't always that way. Like so many people, their true selves are often hidden away when they are with a partner who suppresses what is great about them, and Rob's father was definitely one of those.

The bright and breezy part of Maggie's personality was infectious and lovely to see, but sadly it was something Faye only saw now that she was on the other side of the world, and via computer screen.

"What have you been up to?" Faye asked.

"Not much, if I'm honest. Just chilling out. You?"

"The same. But it's cold, wet and windy here. At least it's nice where you are."

"Twenty-six degrees today, or so the TV says. Might rain though."

"I'll take the rain at twenty-six degrees. When it's six degrees and dark by five o'clock it just makes you miserable."

"Yup."

"So come on, then. How's the big chap?" Maggie asked. "He's out with his pisshead mates again, is he?"

"Every Saturday, but he's not staying out late tonight."

"Has he been fighting?" Maggie asked.

"Not recently. A few weeks back he was walking home and some idiot started on him and knocked the food he was carrying out of his hand. Rob said he just tapped the guy on the chin, on instinct, and the guy was out cold."

"That boy doesn't know his own strength," Maggie said.

"I know. But it worries me. What if the guy had hit his head or something? I know I'm being over-dramatic, but I don't like it."

"Why don't you go out with him?" Maggie asked, causing Faye to shake her head and screw her face up.

"He goes out to have some time to himself," she said.

"Away from you and his boy?"

Faye could see what Maggie was getting at, and had defended him on the subject before.

"I understand it," she said. "I don't disagree with that. It's just the fact that his reputation and his size are a big flashing sign saying 'Fight me!'"

"I know," Maggie said, sadly. "His father was the same, and his reputation's passed down to Rob. That's what happens when you live in a small town: the tough guy's son has to live up to his dad, and people line up to prove themselves against you."

"I don't think I'll ever understand it," Faye said.

"You'll never understand it," Maggie said. "He just has to make sure that it doesn't become all that he is, which is what happened to his father."

"What do you mean?" Faye asked.

"Rob's a sweet guy, right?"

"Of course."

"And he'd never hurt you or Liam, would he?"

"Definitely not," Faye said.

"That's the difference right there. Ken was an angry man from the second he woke up to the moment he went to bed. Rob inherited his size and his power, but he's a good person. He wouldn't go out of his way to hurt someone."

Faye thought about that for a moment.

"I don't like bringing this stuff up. It must bring back awful memories," she said.

Maggie smiled and shook her head.

"I've soaked up enough sun and had plenty of good times since those days," she said. "They're behind me now."

"I'm glad," she said.

"I'll tell you something else, too," Maggie said. "That little boy upstairs in his bed is another giant leap forward for this family escaping its reputation."

"You think?" Faye asked, grinning with pride.

"One hundred and fifty percent," Maggie beamed. "He's the kindest, cutest and cleverest boy I've ever met. You've done a wonderful job raising him, the pair of you."

"Thank you, Maggie. I feel stupid sometimes, seeking reassurance like this. I should just *know*."

"You're a mother, sweetheart. We're all prone to worrying, irrational thoughts and paranoia. But we balance it out with our brilliance and our boobs," Maggie said, bursting into laughter after finishing the sentence.

"You should have that printed on a T-shirt," Faye said.

"I just might," Maggie said.

"Oh, I almost forgot, I have a message for you from Rob."

"Should I be worried?" Maggie asked.

"No. Liam took your email about the koala and turned it into a really cute story. Unfortunately, he then told Rob the true story that influenced it, and Rob was horrified. I'm just giving you a heads-up in case you get a telling off the next time he talks to you."

Maggie laughed.

"We went to a little nature park the other day and a kookaburra stole Roy's sandwich and started laughing at him," she said. "Maybe I'll stick to those kinds of stories in the future?"

"Yeah, I think that's a good idea for now," Faye said.

"For someone so big and strong, he's a bit of wimp, is my son," Maggie said. "More evidence that you don't need to worry about him. He's already shielding Liam from the shittier parts of the world."

"I wanted to ask you about that, too. When do you think is the right time to tell Liam about Ken? A few kids at school have hinted at stuff, and some of the parents have given me looks and made remarks before. It's only a matter of time before he starts hearing stories, and they're almost certainly going to be bullshit."

Maggie bowed her head as she sought the right answer.

"It's a tough one," she said. "He's a mature little monkey, that one. And you're right, he needs to hear the truth from you rather than the extreme version from these mums."

"When shall I do it?" Faye asked.

"Photos are a good idea."

"Photos?"

"Yeah. They're natural conversation starters. When my sister and I used to get together and start going through old photo albums, we'd talk for countless hours about childhood memories, our hopes and fears. Maybe you could do that? Sit down at the table with Rob and Liam, and just let it all pour out. I'm sure Liam'll understand."

"And you don't mind me doing this?" Faye asked.

"Why would I mind? It's all in the past now."

"I'm scared how he's going to react," Faye said.

"Who? Liam or Rob?" Maggie asked.

"Both."

"One thing's for sure: Rob'll never cry. Even as a kid, when Ken was at his worst, Rob would grit his teeth and square his jaw, but he'd never cry," Maggie said, pausing for thought.

"I can remember when Ken came home drunk one day, and he marched into our bedroom full of hate. He called me every name under the sun, and when I called him a coward, he dragged me out of bed by my foot and shouted 'I'm a coward, ey? Who'd fight me, ey?' and I heard a tiny voice behind him say 'I'll fight you, you bastard'. He was eleven years old, and he took a monstrous beating. But he never cried."

The pair sat in silence and stared into their computer screens.

"How do you wake up and get on with life every day?" Faye managed to speak.

"I've had to, and if Rob's ever going to fully step out of Ken's shadow, he's going to have to learn to let it go, before he ends up hurting someone."

Long after the call with Maggie had ended, the words 'hurting someone' were echoing in Faye's ears, and no amount of housework would stop it.

As she washed the day's dishes, filled the washing machine with Liam's school clothes, and generally went about making the house more presentable, she kept thinking about Rob, and a recurring daydream she had where her husband finally cracked and punched somebody to death.

In Faye's mind, she always envisioned it like a scene from a Tarantino or Scorsese film: Slow-motion, the camera pointing up into Rob's snarling face, a seventies soundtrack playing as Rob continued to punch until there was nothing left of the person's face but bloodied flesh.

These daydreams always came about after Maggie talked about the past, which only happened when Rob and Liam weren't around. Maggie had been through years of therapy, and it had made her wonderfully honest about her violent past with Ken, to the point that she could shock the toughest of observers by blurting out a horrendous incident like she was reading a funny headline from a newspaper. Maggie only ever bottled up her past around Rob, because she knew that he didn't want to hear a word of it. Their relationship was strained because of the many things they both witnessed but never spoke about, but only Rob was paying for it now.

Faye finished cleaning and plonked herself down on the sofa with a hot chocolate, topped up with Baileys. It relaxed her and helped her to sleep, and she needed that kind of comfort tonight. She put her feet up and thought about the dimples on Liam's cheeks that appeared whenever he smiled. It managed to drown out the images of violence that were following her through the house.

As she brought her mug up to her lips, Faye caught something out of the corner of her eye. Liam was standing at the door, his hands pressed against the glass, which was something that bugged his mum something rotten. She was prepared to forgive him for it tonight, mainly because he looked so cute in his pyjamas, but also because she was worried how long he had been at the door.

A sleepy Liam pushed open the door as if it was fifty times its weight. His left cheek was reddened from sleeping on his side, and his eyes were adorably heavy. Faye put her mug down on the table and opened her arms. It was all the invitation he needed to jump into them and curl up with her. She kissed his head and rocked him gently.

"Are you alright, beautiful boy?" she asked in a gentle, whispered tone.

"Um-hum," Liam replied.

"Can't sleep?"

Liam shook his head.

"Something on your mind?" she asked.

Liam shrugged his shoulders theatrically.

"Does that mean yes?"

And again.

"You can tell me, y'know?"

Liam squeezed his mum tightly and yawned. His warm breath tickled her neck.

"I love it when you're tired and soppy," Faye said.

She could feel Liam's cheek expand under her chin as it became a big dopey smile.

"Why can't you sleep?" she asked.

"Just thinking," he replied.

"About what?"

"Something Dad said."

"What did he say?" Faye asked, a little anxiously.

"He told me a story Grandma told him about teddy bears coming to life, and now I can't look at Freddy in the same way. He looks scary now."

Faye closed her eyes and tried to contain a smile, kissing Liam on the cheek to prevent herself from laughing and embarrassing Liam.

"Where's Freddy now?" she asked.

"Under the bed. I don't want to look at him."

"Do you want me to get rid of him?" Faye asked.

"No," Liam said, pausing for thought. "Maybe I'll put him in the wardrobe or something."

"Until you feel safer?"

"Uh-huh."

"Good idea."

Faye loved these little moments with Liam, but she was also careful not to mollycoddle him too much, even if it was incredibly difficult to let him go. She reluctantly loosened her grip on him, which was her way of letting him know that cuddle time was coming to an end. Liam slid down the sofa and stood with his shoulders slumped as he prepared to go back to bed.

"Want me to come and tuck you in?" Faye asked, still fighting the urge not to just grab him and hold him until morning.

"No, it's OK," Liam yawned. Heading back to the stairs, he turned back to face his mum.

"How was Grandma?" he asked.

Faye was grabbing her mug back from the coffee table, and she nearly dropped it when Liam asked the question. It was now likely that he had heard everything.

"She's alright, bless her. You know Grandma," she said.

Liam yawned and waved feebly to his mum as he zombie-walked back to his bedroom. With Freddy now stuffed uncomfortably under his bed, Liam was back in the land of nod within two minutes.

Faye thought about the repercussions that might occur from Liam having heard any of her Skype call with Maggie, but after checking on Liam twenty minutes later and finding him snoring away, she concluded that it couldn't have been that traumatic an experience, and left him alone to dream.

8

The Goat was packed to the rafters from 8:30pm on a Saturday, and split into three sections: the regulars, the public schoolers and college students section, and the old-men-who-have-been-here-since-it-opened. These sections kept clear of each other until around 10pm when the trouble started and the place resembled a battle scene from *Braveheart*, minus the face paint and kilts.

The interior of The Goat was that of a pub where the landlord had decided to turn it into a wine bar/club, but had run out of money halfway through, leaving an area for a DJ to set up next to an old fashioned jukebox and three fruit machines. The walls had been painted white because the landlord had read somewhere that it kept the punters thinking it was earlier in the night, because it made the room lighter.

The floorboards were hard oak and heavy duty, and they had to be, as the amount of beer that had spilled on them over the years was legendary. Not to mention the number of rumbles and stampedes there had been, from drunken brawls to police raids.

The pub was closed down for eighteen months after an undercover police investigation lead to a raid that saw seventy percent of the clientele arrested for drug possession. It would've reopened the next day, had it not been for the landlord that was selling the class A's from behind the counter.

With new ownership came no turnaround, and it was unlikely that the pub was ever going to change. The police viewed it as a holding pen these days, and the attitude was very much 'if they're in there, they're not bothering anyone else', which was the police's way of saying 'we don't have the time or the manpower to sort this shit out, so just stay clear of the place.'

A few months back, a kid was arrested for spray painting 'Enter at your own risk' on the wall outside. It wasn't Banksy, but it was a fair warning.

Jamie Sampson was going through his daily ritual of telling violent stories from the town's rich history, to anybody who would sit with him long enough to listen.

Rob sat with him at a small table that was nailed to the floor, to prevent it from being thrown at somebody. Jamie was talking to a couple of teenagers who had come over to borrow a lighter, and ended up staying for two pints' worth of storytelling.

"I was going out with this girl, Paula Young. We used to call her Senza Una Donna as a pisstake," he said, confusing the kids with his eighties reference.

"She put it about a bit, but I was obsessed with her, so much so that I challenged the twat she was seeing to a fight. He was some big lad from Leicester, and back then, as teenagers, we thought that because you were from a city, you must be harder than us townies."

Rob stared into the middle distance. He wasn't listening to Jamie's story. For a start, he'd heard it a million times, and secondly, he was thinking about what Faye had said to him before he'd left the house. It was because of that he'd only drank one and a half pints, compared to Jamie's three.

The young lads lapped up Jamie's story as he continued.

"So like a melon, I challenge this guy and all his mates to come down from Leicester and meet my mates, not realising that Rob here – and a few others – had all fucked off on holidays and whatnot. I thought 'Ah, shit', and started pulling together the best crew I could possibly find, which consisted of the kid I babysat for on weekends and two guys who couldn't crack a rice crispy with their hardest punch."

The two lads turned to each other and laughed.

"Anyway, I had no choice but to bring a baseball bat to the fight, just to even up the odds a bit. The guys came off the train and met us on a patch of green near the station, and I tried to pull the baseball bat out of my trousers and it got stuck in my belt and wouldn't come out, and my crew all legged it down the street, leaving me on my own."

"Shit... What happened?" asked Zach, the younger of the two lads.

"The cops came and parted us before anything kicked off," Jamie said, which disappointed the audience.

"What? That's it?" asked Rich, the older of the two.

"Nope," Jamie said. "The Leicester lads were told to do one by the police, and they did. Then the cops turned to me and said, 'Are you alright, son?' I was like, 'Yes officers, I'm fine,' and all that shit. One of the cops says, 'Be on your way, then.'"

Jamie pointed down at his leg, and the two lads perked up again.

"I've got a fucking baseball bat stuck down my leg," he said.

The two lads started laughing.

"How was I going to get away from the police without looking like Lee Evans in *There's Something about Mary*? I stood there for a minute and nodded along, pretending to get my breath back. But the police wouldn't go. They stood there and waited. And waited. And waited. And waited. It was awkward."

"What did you do, shit your pants and run?" asked Zach.

"I waited it out until they got back in their car and left, and then limped off around the corner and sorted myself out."

The two lads shook their heads and finished their beers off.

"Well played, sir," Rich said. "You stuck it out. Fair play to you."

"Yeah, it worked," Jamie continued. "But from that point on, those cops thought I was a bit special. They'd stop me every time they saw me and ask me if I was alright, and if I needed a lift home. It became embarrassing, so I took action."

Rob leant forward and finished off his pint. It was the part of the story he didn't like to hear.

"When this chap came back from his holidays, we went round to Paula's house and gave those Leicester lads the kicking of all kickings. They never came back again, and when the cops found out about it, they arrested me and normal service was resumed."

"And did you get it on with Paula?" asked Zach, excited at the thought of hearing a sordid-yet-happy ending.

"No," Jamie barked, screwing his face up like he'd used dog shit instead of toothpaste. "She was shagging anything with meat and a pulse, and she's a fat tramp now with six kids from four different dads."

The two lads were confused.

"I thought the whole point of the story was that you beat the lads up so that you could get with Paula?" asked Zach.

Pause.

The longest amount of time that Jamie had ever been quiet.

"Oh yeah," he said, and burst into laughter.

Zach and Rich turned to each other and did the telepathic 'let's get out of here' look that all good friends know how to pull out when the time is right to leave.

"Cool, so yeah, we're gonna shoot off, I think," Rich said, in the most awkward and unnatural way possible.

"Nice one gents," Jamie said, and put out his hand for the two youngsters to shake, which they dutifully did. "Catch you in here again sometime, I hope."

"Yeah, definitely," Zach said, and they left the pub.

Jamie turned to Rob and grinned.

"Remember when we were that age?" he said.

"Unfortunately," Rob replied.

"What's up with you tonight? You're in a right arse."

"I'm not really feeling it tonight, to be honest," Rob said, twisting his pint glass in its own condensation as he stared at the table.

"What's on your mind, bud?" Jamie asked, turning to face his friend.

"Nothing really, just something that Faye said."

Rob's voice trailed off, and Jamie took a deep breath.

"I don't mean to be a dick, but Faye and Julie are both very much alike, in that they are a bit on the naggy-bitch side," he said, sitting back a little in expectation of retaliation from Rob.

Rob stopped playing with his glass and sat back.

"It's not nagging, she's got a point," he said. "She wants me to talk to Liam about my dad before anyone else gets there first."

"I see," Jamie said, clearing his throat. "And you don't think the little bugger's ready for that talk just yet?"

"No, I don't think he is. And I don't know how I would tell him anyway. I mean," Rob took a breath to gather his thoughts. "You remember what he was like?"

"I do. I do."

"Would you tell Carl if your dad was like that?"

"My dad was softer than a pillow made of shite," Jamie said. "But I get what you mean. Do you tell him what he was like to you, or what he was like to your ma?"

"Exactly."

"I gotta tell you, mate, I'd just tell him everything. Get it all out there. See what happens. What's the worst that can happen? He'll see your mum in a different way – and he doesn't see her anyway – and he'll understand you better. I can't see a downside, except for you, because I know you're not the type to open up like that. It'll be hard, mate."

"Can you remember what he was like?" Rob asked.

Jamie's cheeky-chappy exterior turned serious in a split-second as he thought back to his schooldays as Rob's closest friend.

"Mate, he was terrifying," he said. "I remember calling round for you once, and your dad let me in the house. He put his arm around me and asked me how I was as he took me to the stairs and sent me up to see you. As he guided me to the stairs, I looked through a crack in the door frame and saw your mum sitting on a chair in the middle of the kitchen. She had her face in her hands, and it was clear to me that your dad had moved me through the house as quickly as possible so I wouldn't see her. He knew I'd always stop and talk to her, and she clearly wasn't in a state to do that."

Rob stared into his empty pint glass.

"How do you explain stuff like that to a kid?" he asked.

"You just do it, mate. Don't write it out. Don't rehearse it. Don't even stop to think about it. Just tell it as you saw it. Because if it ends up being some dickhead like me telling the story... Well, you heard that shit I was talking to those kids. You don't want Liam listening to your story told like that, by people who'll just as easily make out like you're the same, when you couldn't be further removed from that bastard if you tried."

Rob's face lit up. He needed to hear that, especially from his friend.

"I've got to ask you one question though," Jamie said. "And you're not going to like it. But it's an important one."

Rob nodded his approval for Jamie to continue with his line of questioning.

"Have you ever raised your hand to Liam in his life?" Jamie asked.

The blood flowed fast to Rob's cheeks, but he knew that it was an important question to be asked.

"I've never so much as told him off. Let alone raise my hand to him."

"Then you've got nothing to worry about," he said, relieved. "You're not one of these 'my father did this to me, so I'm going to do it to my kids' types. Those people piss me off. We're not programmed to repeat the same mistakes as the people who raised us. That's bullshit. You make sure Liam appreciates that when you tell him everything your father did. Understand?"

"Yes mate, and thanks," Rob said, almost in a whisper. "I'm sorry for ruining your night with serious talk."

"Don't be ridiculous," Jamie said, perking up again. "Within two hours there'll be chair legs, glasses and bodies being thrown around in here, and I'll be back to being a dickhead again. Why don't you go home and give Faye a little cuddle, ey? She's probably beating herself up about this, too."

Rob grabbed Jamie's head, pulling it towards him and planting a kiss on top of it. Jamie laughed and quickly restyled his hair, not that it made the slightest bit of difference to his rapidly balding head.

"I'll catch up with you soon," Rob said.

"Take it easy, mate."

It was the first time that Rob had left The Goat before 9pm on a Saturday in months, and it felt strange to walk down the darkened street in which it stood without some kind of carnage unfolding. He had much more of a bounce in his step now that he'd managed to get some of his feelings off his chest, and as the sign for The Golden Fleece came into view and his stomach started to rumble, he looked forward to sharing his bed with Faye and making it up to her for being such a closed shop about his past.

9

Andy and Ben were pretty drunk. Their eyes were glazed, their words slurred and their cheeks red from the warmth of the pub and the alcohol in their systems. Charlie scanned the main section of his pub, which was vastly depleted of customers and winding down for the evening. Gail was stocking the fridges behind him.

The two Londoners, Ray and Clive, were still seated at the bar, and weren't making for an easy atmosphere. Clive's headgear was a disturbing distraction and the elephant in the room, and Ray's tendency to stare at people wasn't likely to endear himself to the locals any time soon.

Charlie approached the pair as Clive slurped the last part of his pint through his straw like a milkshake.

"Can I get you some more Dutch courage, gents?" he asked.

"Yes, please," Ray said.

"Thamks," Clive slurred.

"You're more than welcome," Charlie said, and gave them both a warm smile before pouring two pints.

Ray rolled his eyes and stared at his friend.

"You're starting to slur your words," he said.

"Sowwy," Clive said, drowsily. "The meds are mixing with the alcowol."

"Shut the fuck up talking then. It's embarrassing."

Charlie put the two pints down on the bar and backed away with his hands up.

"These are on me, lads," he said.

Ray lifted his glass to Charlie. Clive nodded his appreciation and swapped pints with his straw. Ray could feel Andy and Ben looking at his friend, so instead of trying to catch them out, he thought he'd communicate in another way.

"His cheekbone and jaw were shattered, and he bit the end of his tongue off," Ray said, without looking up.

Charlie, presuming that Ray was talking to him, did what any good landlord or polite person would do, and gave Clive a sympathetic smile.

"Very sorry to hear that, sir. I hope you get better soon," he said, before turning to help Gail with the fridges. Gail locked eyes with her husband and gave him the 'what a stupid thing to say' look, and Charlie closed his eyes and nodded, agreeing with her.

Andy and Ben ignored Ray's revelation and carried on talking rubbish as usual. Their childish banter would normally be ignored, but the pub was so quiet and the atmosphere so tense that every time Ben guffawed or Andy scraped his stool across the floor, the noise was amplified a thousand times, and the slightest sound crept up Charlie's spine like a child being told a ghost story.

Charlie had been in the game long enough to be able to tell the difference between tourists and out-of-towners looking for trouble, and he had Ray and Clive pegged as the latter.

Ben leant back and let out a huge laugh, and almost fell off his stool as a result. The sound was enough for Charlie to rise from the fridges and march over to the pair.

"Did I not tell you to quieten down? It's like the bloody war room in Washington in here. Something is going to kick off, I can feel it," he whispered, albeit aggressively.

"Calm down, Charlie. Viagra's making you paranoid, man!" Ben said, nudging Andy, who let out a giggle.

"How did you—" Charlie paused mid-sentence, realising that he'd let his guard down a little too far in his panic. "Bastards."

Andy and Ben broke into hysterics as an embarrassed Charlie turned around and started to wander off.

"A little too confessional there, Charlie," Ben called out. "Don't worry though, we won't tell anyone."

A rattled Charlie span around and pointed at the red-faced pair.

"I don't want you fanny-farting any more cruel things about anyone. I've had enough of you and your mouth. Drink up and piss off if you're going to continue," he said.

Ben sat more upright in his chair and pretended to straighten a tie in an attempt to look civilised.

"I deeply apologise," he said. "From now on, I will be like a character from one of those clever books from school."

"'Roger Red Hat'?" Andy chimed in.

"Very funny. No. The ones that the BBC always make for the grannies to watch on a Sunday teatime?"

"Jane Austen," Charlie said.

"Yep, that's the one. *The Three Musketeers* and the like."

Charlie and Andy looked at each other. Andy leapt off his stool for the toilet again.

"You're pissing like a racehorse!" Ben laughed.

Andy made an impression of a horse as he made his way to the men's room. Ben watched as he passed Tony, who must have been suffering from severe heat sickness by now. He was still fast asleep.

"Rest your balls on Tony's face and I'll take a photo," Ben called out to Andy as he passed him.

"Fuck that," Andy shouted back. "I'll get third degree burns."

Charlie poured a pint of water and took it over to Tony. He kicked the chair to startle sleeping beauty awake, and passed the water down to him.

"Have some water, Tony. You must have a mouth like a desert," he said.

"Lawrence of Arabia," Tony replied, taking the pint and downing it within a few seconds.

"You should probably get home, Tony. Want me to call you a taxi?"

Tony's wild eyes circled the room like they were following a fly. When it hit him that he wasn't actually *at* home, he stood up quickly and stormed out of the pub without saying a word.

Ray and Clive were more than a little bemused as they watched the strange drama unfold.

"That's the kind of people you have around here is it?" Ray asked.

"Aye," Charlie said, gathering up Tony's empties and taking them back to the bar with him. "Let's just say it's an eclectic mix."

"I don't suppose one of your eclectic customers goes by the name of Rob Thomas?" he sneered.

Like a dog hearing his master's key hitting the front door, Ben's ears pricked up and his back straightened, and Charlie was riddled with anxiety. He didn't want to lie to them, but he didn't want any trouble either.

"Rob Thomas? Aye, we see him in here from time to time," he said.

"Tonight?" Ray asked, his eyes locking on Charlie like a professional poker player looking for a tell.

"He hasn't been in here tonight, no."

"Do you think he will?" Ray asked.

"I doubt it."

"Where would he go on such a fine evening?"

Ben watched Charlie capitulating to Ray's intimidating presence and didn't like it one bit. He necked his pint and let out one of the loudest burps known to mankind. It was enough to make the married couple enjoying white wine spritzers by the window to get up and leave, and enough for Ray to turn his attention to Ben.

"What about you, Belcher?" he asked. "Do you know Rob?"

Ben had a smug grin on his face, and he gave Charlie a quick look as if to say 'let me handle this' before facing Ray.

"I do indeed. I taught him everything he knows," he said.

"Is that right?" Ray asked, grinning.

"Yep," Ben said, then waved his empty glass to Charlie, who started pouring another for him. "I taught him the magical art of the somerflip, and he perfected it on your mate's big metal chin."

Clive launched himself out of his stool, but Ray put his hand on his shoulder and eased him back down. Charlie finished pouring Ben's latest pint and put it down in front of him.

"You can drink that, then piss off," he said.

Ben seemed more hurt at the prospect of being kicked out than he was afraid of Ray and Clive, but that might have been because of the level of alcohol in his system. As a man who was still afraid of spiders, he was hardly the toughest man in town.

"I won't be having any trouble here tonight," Charlie said, pointing at both groups.

Gail put a reassuring arm around her husband's waist.

"*We* won't put up with it," Gail said.

Ray nodded to the landlords, then stood and approached Ben, who crept more and more into his shell the closer he got. Charlie and Gail watched Ray closely as he sat in Andy's seat. He held out his hand for Ben to shake.

"No hard feelings, mate," he said.

Ben swallowed, then placed his hand into Ray's slowly, like he was afraid that Ray was holding an electric shock buzzer. Ray squeezed Ben's hand as he shook it, and Ben gritted his teeth as they made their peace. When Ray let go, Ben hid his hand under the bar and flicked his wrist to get the circulation back, and Ray went back to his stool.

"I think you'd better leave after that pint, gents," Charlie said.

"Fair enough, landlord. We weren't staying anyway. Like I said, we're just looking for Rob Thomas, and my inebriated friend here knows why."

Charlie's eyes flitted across to Ben, who was working out what 'inebriated' meant. He was now regretting the 'somerflip' comment.

"Yeah, we wash there," Clive slurred, staring at Ben.

"What's that got to do with knowing where he is?" Charlie said, sticking up for his loyal patron.

"It's a small town, and they were walking home together. Makes sense that he'd know where he lives, or at least where he drinks," Ray said.

"Even if he knew, do you think he'd tell you?" Charlie asked.

"Why wouldn't he?" Ray asked.

"No offence, friend, but look at your friend's head. I'm guessing that it was Rob that did that, and it looks pretty nasty, but it doesn't mean that we're going to give him up to you. It's not the way this works. Small town or big city, we don't screw over our own."

Ray laughed and took a swig from his pint.

"That's very honourable of you, big man," he said. "Funny how the police who came to visit my friend in hospital thought differently. We only know his name because they were so keen on us to press charges. Sounds like he makes a habit of this kind of thing."

Ben's face was turning a lighter shade of white by the second, and couldn't cope with the intensity in the air any longer.

"What are you going to do to Rob?" he blurted out.

Ray put his hand into his coat pocket and pulled out a white envelope.

"Nothing sinister, mate. We're slapping him with the medical bill for what he did to my friend Clive here," he said, followed by a laugh. "You've been watching too many Danny Dyer films, chaps. No need for violence."

"Who said anything about violence?" Ben said.

"Well, your Scottish friend looks pretty anxious right now, and your leg's shaking like a one-legged gymnast on a very slim beam. Don't you think my friend's face is a good enough reason for some violent retribution?"

The big words were killing Ben.

"Violet metro..."

"For God's sake, Ben!" Charlie shouted. He'd had enough now, and made sure that Ray knew it.

"You can hardly blame us for thinking along violent lines," he said. "That man's used to having to fight his way through life. When you're a big bastard, everyone wants a crack at you."

"Never understood that myself," Ray said. "You wouldn't fight a heavyweight if you were a lightweight would you? Seems a little daft."

"Why else would you spend your life getting pissed and fighting? Of course they're daft. They're fucking idiots."

Ray nodded in agreement and finished the rest of his pint.

"If you want to find Rob, you should try The Goat on Elizabeth Road," Charlie said, causing Ben to sit up in amazement. "Just head out of here and down the next street and you'll find it in no time. By this time of the night, that's where most people are going, so just follow the hordes of Polo shirts or the smell of perfume."

"The Goat? It's a pub?" Ray asked.

"It's the main pub in town. A big shithole full of mouthy morons carrying bottles of WKD under their sleeves in case somebody looks at them funny. I won't be having any fighting or intimidation here. This is a public house, not Guantanamo Bay."

"Don't they torture people in that place?" Ray asked.

Charlie's patience had well and truly worn out.

"I don't want any torture here either!" he said, raising his voice.

Clive nudged Ray with his elbow and finished off his pint through his straw.

"Maywe we shour goo ta tha goat pwace?" he said, well and truly caned from the beer and painkiller combination.

"Maybe you should stop munching on painkillers like they're Smarties and shut the fuck up?"

Ben giggled, causing Ray to turn to him and give him the death stare. Ben buttoned it instantly. Ray stood up and held out his hand to Charlie.

"You've got a cosy little establishment here, Charlie," he said. "And a lovely wife. I didn't catch your name, love?"

"Gail," she said.

"Hello, Gail."

Ray put his hand away when it became clear that Charlie wasn't going to shake it in a million years.

"Thanks for your help, Charlie. If he's not in The Goat, we might return with our papers. Don't suppose there's any hope of us getting his home address?" he asked.

"Bob Hope."

"Thought not," he said, smiling. He turned to a drowsy looking Clive and nudged him into life. "Come on, sleepy head. We've got a goat to visit."

Clive stood up and groggily left the bar area with Ray, who stopped at the door.

"See you around, boys and girls."

He closed the door behind them.

"What was in that sports bag?" Ben asked.

Charlie shook his head.

"I don't know, and I don't want to know."

Andy arrived back at his seat. He noticed that everybody looked like they'd been through hell.

"Somebody die in the time I was gone?" he asked.

"Where were you when I needed you? You're supposed to be my best friend and look out for me," Ben said.

"I was having a poo. What did I miss?"

Ben shook his head and looked away, leaving Charlie to explain.

"I think Rob Thomas might be in a bit of trouble tonight," he said, sombrely. "I'd advise you both to stay the hell away from The Goat."

The warning had no effect on Andy, who became more animated at the thought of seeing some action.

"Rob's going to be in a fight? Get in! What time?" he asked.

Gail shook her head and started clearing the bar and empty tables. She'd heard quite enough macho bullshit for one evening.

"They're not meeting at the crack of dawn with pistols," Charlie said.

"That would be pretty cool," Andy said. "Entertaining. Anyway, Rob usually goes to The Goat at about eight. What's the time now?"

"Half nine," Ben said. "Do you think we should warn him?"

"And miss a perfectly good somerflip? No way! I'm not missing that again."

Charlie had reached breaking point.

"Be quiet!" he shouted.

Silence.

Andy dragged his foot, desperately trying to contain his excitement but eager not to be growled at by Charlie again. Charlie now had a second to think, and he had an idea.

"Ben's right, we should warn him," he said. "I'm ringing Mark at The Goat. Maybe he can sneak Rob out the back door before they get there?"

Andy was disgusted with Ben for depriving him of his great opportunity.

"Pop your nuts back out from inside yourself and get your phone at the ready," he said, giving Ben a pep talk that wasn't quite Mickey-to-Rocky, but it was inspiring enough to make the hairs on the back of Ben's neck stand on end.

"Think about it, man," he continued. "If we can get a video of Rob somerflipping a cockney on your phone, it'll be huge. Or even better…"

"We'll be rich?" Ben said, optimistically.

"Nah, don't be silly. *You've Been Framed*."

Ben responded like Jesus had appeared in front of him. His eyes widened and his mouth gaped open. The sound of Charlie dialling out on the pub's phone broke him out of his daydream though, and he leant over the bar to try and grab Charlie and stop him from calling Mark at The Goat.

"Stop! Stop! Stop! Stop!" he cried out as he stretched over.

Charlie took one step to the right to get out of Ben's reach, and started to speak to Mark on the phone, ignoring Ben.

"Hi mate, is Rob there...? Thank Christ for that... Oh, the usual... Two London blokes looking for him... Yep... Yep... I know... His dad... Exactly the same... Twat... Twat..."

Charlie looked over to Andy and Ben, who was still hanging over the bar but had giving up trying to grab him.

"Twats," he said.

Charlie put the phone down, grabbed a beer mat and slapped Ben around the head with it. He swatted him back behind the bar.

"Piss off back there, you troublemaking little shitbag," he said.

"Ah, c'maaaan, Charlie," Andy said. "You can't blame us for wanting to see a bit of action on a Saturday night."

"I can blame myself. I *do* blame myself."

"Then why did you tell the cockneys where The Goat was?" Ben asked.

"Because I didn't want them here, and I never want them back here. Rob's big enough to take care of himself."

"But you said you wouldn't give him up?" Ben said, becoming more confused by the second.

"Yeah, well, I did my bit," Charlie said, and glanced over to Gail, who was wiping down tables and looking deflated.

"What did Mark say?" Andy said.

"Rob was there earlier but he's left now. Hopefully he's at home, and no drunk idiot tells those Londoners where he lives."

"Do you think they really have a medical bill, Charlie?" Ben asked.

"Who has a medical bill, Ben?" Charlie said, embarrassed that Ben had to ask. "We have a service called the NHS in this country."

Charlie drifted into thought. He knew that he'd done the right thing, getting rid of the men by telling them about The Goat. He was thinking of Gail and Katie, and his livelihood. He had a sneaking suspicion that something awful was going to happen, and he wanted no part in it.

Andy and Ben crept off their stools and prepared to leave. Before they could make their way to their ringside seats at The Goat, Charlie mumbled something to himself.

"Just like his old man."

Andy and Ben stopped dead in their tracks.

"Stay with us, Charlie. What do you mean 'just like his old man'?" asked Andy, one arm in his jacket already.

Charlie opened his fridge and took out one of his most expensive beers. He cracked the top off and took a swig, before leaning against the bar.

"Rob's dad was exactly the same. Fortunately, he was dead and buried before you two grew pubic hair and a taste for beer. He was a fighting magnet and a right hard bastard, was Ken Thomas."

"Rob takes after him then?" Ben asked.

"Not in all ways, I hope. Or that young lad of his has got a horrible future ahead of him."

"Why?" Andy asked.

"When Rob and David, his brother, who lives in Scotland now, were nippers, they were left with Ken whilst Maggie, their mum, went out on the razz. Ken was a fun loving guy on the surface, but he could weep or kill at the flip of a coin. He was paranoid, too. Always convinced his wife was sleeping around."

Andy and Ben moved in to listen more carefully.

"Anyway, he lets her go out and he watches the kids. Midnight comes, and Ken's drank himself into a jealous stupor, and his mind is playing tricks on him. Like a kettle, he reaches boiling point, and off he goes."

"Where does he go?" Ben asked, enthralled.

"He storms out of the house and goes looking for his missus, leaving two sleeping infants in their beds. He walks into every pub and scans the room like a bull who's been kicked in the bollocks, putting the frighteners into everyone. I mean, he was scary enough when he was sober, but that night, he was foaming at the mouth and his eyes were black. He was gone."

"Fucking hell," Andy whispered.

"He finds Maggie drinking and giggling with her mates. Innocent fun. Nothing out of the ordinary. He storms over and drags her the mile home by her hair. Of course, he did this *after* he knocked out her best friend after she stood up to him. Meanwhile, a pub full of spineless fellas stared down at their shoes and did nothing."

Gail stopped wiping tables and listened. She couldn't look at her husband for fear that she would burst into tears.

"In the meantime, Rob and David had woken up and come downstairs to an empty house. They found the beer that Ken had left behind and drank the lot. Nine and seven years of age they were, so naturally they were pissed just from smelling the stuff. Anyway, Ken drags Maggie into the house, only to find two drunk kids crying and projectile vomiting around the living room. He slams the front door and for all intents and purposes beats the living shit out of all three of them with this big Clint Eastwood belt that he used to wear."

Andy and Ben flinch at the thought of being smacked by such an object.

"And just when you thought it couldn't get any worse, he goes to kick his wife as she's crawling away and he puts his foot through the TV."

"Where were the fucking police?" Gail asked, barely able to hold back her tears.

"They turned up. They turned up. Ken was standing at the door when the police arrived, a bloodied belt in one hand and a TV stuck to his foot. But nobody pressed charges, so not a lot happened. After that, Maggie didn't go out again until after Ken died."

Silence.

"How do you know all of this, Charlie?" Andy asked.

Charlie sighed and bowed his head.

"I was one of the spineless fellas in the pub."

Ben looked at the saddened faces of Gail, Andy and Charlie, and was starting to get a little bored. A normal human being would've said something reassuring and then used it as a point of departure, but Ben wasn't a normal human being, and he was getting restless.

"I liked the bit about the drunk kids," he said.

The mood was destroyed instantly, and Andy chuckled, albeit remorsefully.

Charlie picked up a bar towel and threw it into Ben's face.

"Get out, you bastard!" he shouted. "Go out and watch another generation destroy itself with violence."

"Good-oh," Ben said, backing away with Andy following.

"See you, Charlie," Andy said, apologetically.

"Can I have a bottle of Stella on tick?" Ben asked.

"GET OUT OF MY PUB!!"

Andy and Ben gathered their wallets, cigarettes and keys together and made it for the exit, muttering under their breath as they left.

"What's up with him all of a sudden?" Ben asked Andy, who was pushing him towards the door. "You let two girls get chinned, not me."

Charlie watched them go, a mixture of anger and built-up regret flowing through his body and boiling his blood. Gail approached the bar and placed the palms of her hands on his cheeks. She forced him to look into her eyes.

"I love you, Charlie Winters," she said. "There was nothing more you could've done that night, and there's nothing more you could've done tonight. People have to be accountable for their own actions."

"I know," Charlie said, sadly. "And I love you, too."

"I can remember when cars filled with goons from the surrounding villages and towns would come down to test themselves against Rob Thomas," Gail said. "And that horrible father of his would lap up every second of it. There's nothing you can do for someone like that, and there's nothing Rob can do about it now."

Charlie nodded, but was somewhere else entirely.

Gail kissed her man on the lips and started clearing the bar area of any trace of Ben, Andy or the two cockneys.

"Just think: two condoms and the world could have been spared," she said.

Charlie laughed.

The door to the pub opened. Tony had come back to pay The Black Bull a visit. He approached the bar with a big daft grin on his face. As soon as Charlie saw him, he smiled. As strange as Tony was, you knew exactly what you were getting with him, and right now, harmless familiarity was exactly what he needed.

"At last, a normal person," Charlie said, with the most excitement he'd shown all day. "What can I get you, you beautiful bastard?"

"Orange juice," Tony said.

Charlie poured him a pint of beer instead, as per usual.

"There you go, my good friend," Charlie said.

Tony took a sip from the pint and winked at Charlie.

Charlie looked over at Gail and they shared a smile. Charlie turned a knob on the wall and faded the lights. It was time to wind down for the night.

10

The Golden Fleece was the most popular Chinese takeaway in town. It sat on the corner of Charles Street, fifty yards from the secondary school and around the corner from the main road. Many drunkards visited The Fleece as they tottered home with a rumbling stomach, and if it wasn't for them, the place would've closed a long time ago. The food was cheap, and its reputation had been tarnished ever since cat meat had allegedly been found by health inspectors. After closing down for a month, the decor was updated and the owner's wife became front-of-house instead of their son, who had started college, but nothing else changed. It didn't stop people eating there, especially after they'd demolished nine pints.

Rob still used The Fleece. It was five minutes from home, and convenience therefore negated any thoughts of feline scandals and the rumour mill flapping their mouths. He figured that until the day their chicken balls stopped tasting nice after being dunked in sweet and sour sauce, he was willing to put any negative thoughts to one side for the sake of his stomach. He was more of a dog person anyway, he would joke with Faye as he munched away.

Shun owned the restaurant, and despite the fact that his name meant 'smooth and agreeable' in his native land, he was anything but. The kids of the town liked to play a game called 'Hit and Run', which consisted of running into the shop, shouting 'cat fuckers' and then running for your life. Shun would chase you to the end of the street with a meat cleaver in his hand and then go back to work, cursing the kids in his native tongue. It was a terrifying and surreal sight to behold if you happened to be passing by, and people joked that whenever Shun changed his menu, missing child posters would suddenly appear throughout the town.

Shun's wife Bao could only just see over the counter in the restaurant. She was a sweet and giggly lady who barely spoke a word of English, but she had mastered numbers, menu items and 'get the fuck out', which came in handy around 11pm on a Friday and Saturday night. A small bell would ring whenever the door of The Fleece opened, and Bao would appear from under the desk, as if she had been conjured from thin air.

Rob entered The Fleece, and Bao gave him a menu. He took a seat and started reading. The takeaway resembled a GP's waiting room, with a half-circle counter and a beaded door separating the counter and the small kitchen out the back, where pots and pans could be heard clattering and oil sizzling for hours on end.

The front consisted of two rows of chairs facing each other, and they were close enough to be as awkward as a doctor's waiting room. The only difference was that you'd spend time trying to figure out what the person had ordered, rather than what was wrong with them.

A large ugly plant that hadn't been watered for months sat on a small table between the two rows of chairs, and a handful of style and celebrity magazines had been flung on top of it about a decade ago. When the front page story of the top magazine is about Brad and Jennifer's tragic split, it's time to update your library.

The only other customer in The Fleece was Eddie Howard, the sixteen year old son of Tony, and a renowned troublemaker. He had been expelled from more schools than most parents knew existed, and he lived to the archetypal product-of-a-broken-home, mainly because he was so fed up of being told he was one.

An opportunist thief with a short attention span, Eddie was the kind of kid that was endearingly goofy, and whose boundless energy could've been put to good use, if anybody could be in a room with him for more than five minutes without having their wallet stolen.

Eddie was rubbing his hands on his knees and rocking back and forth like a heroin addict. It reminded Rob of the scene in *Trainspotting* where Spud goes for a job interview whilst on amphetamines. Eddie and Spud had a lot in common. They were both lovable rogues. They'd nick the fillings out of their grandmother's teeth, but it wouldn't mean they didn't love them.

Rob quickly passed the stage of being amused by Eddie's erratic behaviour to feeling a little awkward. He felt the need to break the ice before Eddie started smashing the room up or something.

"You're Tony Howard's son, aren't you?" he asked.

"Yes I am," Eddie said, twitching. "And I'm bursting for me lemon chicken. Fifteen minutes I've been waiting. There's nobody else here."

"There's probably a backlog of telephone orders," Rob said.

"The phone hasn't rang once since I've been here."

"I can't help you then, mate. Why don't you read a magazine?"

"They used to have a TV in here. They must have traded it for some shaved cats."

"They must have employed you to drum up business," Rob said, sarcastically. "Talking to you is really making me hungry."

"I'm sorry. I have a beautiful girl waiting for me, and she wants lemon chicken. And I want her knick-knacks. So excuse me if I am coming across as anxious, because I am extremely anxious."

Eddie rocked a little quicker, before standing up to look over the counter. Bao was in the kitchen helping out her husband, not hiding from Eddie on her small chair.

"Maybe you should ask them to hurry up?" Rob asked.

"They only understand the numbers on the side of their dishes on the menu," Eddie replied.

Rob sat up in his chair and gave Eddie a disapproving look.

"Sorry, sorry," Eddie said, calming down slightly.

Rob waited for Eddie to settle down again, like a hunter waiting for a tranquilliser dart to take effect.

"How's your dad anyway?" he asked, attempting to take Eddie's attention away from his lemon chicken.

"Still a bastard," Eddie shot back. "He hit me with his Harley Davidson belt the other day. Big bastard buckle on it. I've gotta walk around with 'Harley' and 'Davidson' written on my arse cheeks. Only it looks like his name is Harley 'O' Davidson now, on account of me arsehole."

Rob tried to smother a laugh but couldn't manage it.

"You're a funny one," he sniggered.

"If you don't laugh at life's little depressions, what can you do?" he replied.

"You have a point, Eddie. You have a point."

Both men stared into space for a short while. Rob considered reading a celebrity magazine from 2006, but Eddie broke the silence.

"Why do dads always use belts?" Eddie mumbled, as much to himself as to Rob.

"I don't know," Rob replied, the memories flooding back to him. "A quick and easy way to inflict maximum pain on misbehaving kids, I guess."

"Yeah, I guess," Eddie said, drifting off. "What belt did your dad use?"

"I don't think it had a brand, it just had a big fuck-off buckle on it. Looked like a heavyweight championship of the world belt. Massive thing."

"Ouch," Eddie grimaced. "I'm never gonna use a belt on my kids."

"Me neither."

"I'll use harsh language, and the naughty step," he continued. "I don't like aggression."

Eddie paused for a moment, then charged up to the desk, slamming the palms of his hands on the counter.

"Oi! Where's my lemon chicken!" he shouted, before turning back to Rob with a look of concern on his face. "Stick up for me, Rob. My mate called Shun a cat killer the other day and he chased him with a fuck-off knife the size of me leg."

Rob sat up in panic.

"Don't get me involved in your shit!" he said.

Bao emerged from her beaded curtain and grinned at Eddie.

"What is noise?" Bao asked.

"I've been waiting sixteen minutes and forty-six seconds for me lemon chicken!" Eddie said.

"All cooked fresh. Many orders out back. Soon."

Rob had never heard Bao say more than a few words of English before, and it made him smile. If he worked at The Fleece, he wouldn't want the morons that ate there to know that he spoke English either.

The bell at the door jingled, and a burly man in his sixties approached the counter. Bao met him with a smile and went into the kitchen to fetch his order. As the man paid and waited for his change, Eddie's rage boiled from his toes to his eyelids, and he made a couple of strange noises as his self-control did battle with his anger.

The customer left the takeaway with his food, and Eddie could contain himself no longer.

"This is favouritism!" he yelled. "I demand prawn crackers!"

Bao ignored Eddie and focused on taking Rob's order with her tiny pad and pen.

"Hi, I'll have a number six, a number forty-two, two number sevens and a twenty-one. Thanks."

"Fifteen minutes, take seat."

"Cheers."

Bao went into the kitchen with Rob's order, which was written on a post-it note in Chinese symbols.

"Don't pass through the beads without agreeing to the complimentary crackers," Eddie yelled to Bao, who rightfully ignored him.

"I love Chinese writing," Rob said, smiling to himself.

"I love battered chicken balls smothered in lemon sauce, but we can't have the moon on a stick," Eddie said, as petulant and impatient as ever. "Fifteen minutes for your five dishes. Seventeen minutes and counting for mine. Are they growing the lemons before cooking the chicken?"

Rob shook his head and shrugged his shoulders, and sat back down in his chair. Eddie was looking increasingly desperate now. His face was screwed up and his leg was twitching, like a child needing the toilet. No wonder that the kid had found himself in trouble with schools and the police so often. He had the attention span of a gnat.

"No sex without lemon chicken," he muttered to himself, before slamming himself into a chair and folding his arms.

Rob laughed, but Eddie was speedily warring on him.

"Christ mate, you're like a junkie," he said.

"I am a junkie! I'm a junkie for girls! And I'm in need of my next fix!" Eddie said, almost in tears. "I'm going to start using Woks Going On. It's more expensive but they don't piss you about. Bollocks to The Golden Fleece! Golden Fleece is a bloody Greek name anyway."

"I think they just liked the name, and you've thought about this *way* too much," Rob said.

"Anything to take my mind off the lemon chicken, or lack of!" Eddie said, gritting his teeth like a man in pain. "Or the lack of sex I'll be getting tonight. The more time I spend here, the less chance I've got of getting some muffin."

Rob tried to sympathise with the poor lad, despite the fact that he was embarrassed that he'd used the term 'muffin' in relation to sex.

"If she's the right girl, I'm sure she will understand," he said.

It was the most generic response he could think to use in order to take Eddie's attention away from his problems, and it seemed to have a calming influence on the lad. He settled down and grinned at Rob.

"What?" Rob asked, as Eddie stared at him like he was a rare bird.

"You're a nice one. More than I thought you'd be," Eddie said.

"What do you mean by that?" Rob asked, as he broke into a frown and leant forward in his seat.

Eddie became flustered and more than a little intimidated. He sat back and started fidgeting, looking anywhere but at the slightly peeved man-mountain in front of him.

"I didn't mean to be a dick, but… well, y'know…" he stuttered.

"No. I don't. That's why I asked," Rob replied, abruptly.

"Y'know. You hear stories. About you, like."

"Don't shit your pants, Eddie. Just say what you've got to say."

"People tell stories about you. About how you knock people sparko quite often. People are afraid of you," Eddie said.

"Are you afraid of me?" Rob asked.

"You *are* a big fella," Eddie said.

"Is that a good enough reason to be afraid of me?"

"It is when you hear the stories. My mate Richard told me that he saw you hit a guy on top of a hill, and they fell to the bottom of the hill without touching the ground," he said, acting out the story like he was showing it on a map.

"That's ridiculous," Rob laughed.

"They flew," Eddie continued, as if Rob didn't understand what he meant.

"Don't worry, I got it," Rob said, sarcastically. "They did come off the floor, but they rolled a few times before hitting the bottom. What your little friend missed out of that story is that the guy had swung for me with a baseball bat."

"Yeah, to be fair, he missed that bit out and went straight to the flying bit."

Rob sighed and sat back in his chair.

"I was talking to the missus about this earlier," Rob said, sadness in his voice.

"About flying?" Eddie asked, confused.

"No. Not about flying."

"I love flying. I want to do a sky dive for my eighteenth birthday," Eddie said, trailing off into his thoughts. Then he remembered why he was still in the room.

"I should have my fucking lemon chicken by then," he continued, and hurled himself up to the counter again, slapping his hands on the marble surface like a performing seal.

"Hello! Hello!" he called out.

From behind Eddie, the door opened again. The jingle of the bell failed to warn Eddie of the incoming punch to the back, which caused him cry out in a high-pitched squeal as he grimaced in pain. Eddie turned around to be faced with Charlie and Gail's daughter, Katie.

"Oww! You could have snapped my spine!" he shrieked, rubbing his back.

"I should snap your cock off! What the hell are you still doing here?" she said.

"I'm waiting for your lemon chicken! Although I'm not sure I should be now, as I have spinal injuries."

"Don't take the piss," she said. "I could be at a birthday party right now, but I blew it off for you! And you're wasting my precious time."

"I'm waiting for your food," Eddie said, his voice reaching the highest it had been since his balls had dropped.

"Why am I always attracted to scruffy arseholes?" Katie asked herself. A good question, judging by the level of attractiveness between the pair. Eddie looked like he had got dressed in a pig pen in the dark, whereas Katie turned heads wherever she went.

Rob was trying hard to look anywhere else but at the feuding lovers, and was also holding in a laugh. He let out a small cough, which caught Katie's attention. She recognised him and sat down next to him.

"Hello, Rob," she said, flirtatiously invading his personal space.

"Hi, Katie," Rob said, leaning away from her.

"Are you coming to the pub later?" she asked.

"Not tonight. Just getting some grub for me and Faye before going home."

"That's sweet. It must be nice for her not to be married to a bellend," she said, causing Rob to bow his head and smile.

"She might argue with you on that one," Rob said.

Eddie was caught between slamming his fists into the counter again and giving up on the girl he loved altogether.

"Bless. Make sure you come and say hello to me next time you're out," Katie said, one eye checking up on Eddie's reaction as she chatted with Rob and leant towards him. "I'll be there a lot more after tonight on account of this twat failing the simplest of tasks."

Eddie attempted to laugh along like he was in on the joke, but it was painful to watch, and Rob felt for him.

"I will, Katie. Now give the boy a chance, yeah? He's a good kid," he said.

Katie turned to Eddie, who was standing still and grinning like an eager kid waiting to be picked for the football team. Katie sneered at him with her mouth, but her eyes couldn't lie. He was an adorably pathetic creature, and she liked him.

Before they could say anything, Bao arrived from the kitchen and presented Eddie with his lemon chicken. It might as well have been the Holy Grail, and Eddie threw his arms in the air like he'd just scored the World Cup winning goal.

"Finally!" he said. "Twenty minutes and no prawn crackers. I won't be coming back here again."

Bao didn't understand him enough to give a damn. She priced the food up on the world's oldest till and put out her hand.

"Three pound twenty," she said.

"How much?" Eddie shrieked.

"Three pound twenty," Bao repeated.

Eddie's hand rummaged through the pockets of his jeans, and then his black zip-up hoodie. His eyes shot across to Rob as he realised that he had no money.

"Erm," he stalled. "Babe…"

Eddie turned to Katie, who could see that Eddie was short on cash as well as brain cells. She slammed a handful of coins on the counter and stormed off towards the exit.

"Babe, babe," Eddie pleaded, unsure whether to leave the food and cash for his girlfriend or stay behind. His hesitation had cost him a night of passion.

"The night's still young," he cried out, in a last-ditch effort to make Katie stay.

"Enjoy your lonely wank, then," she shouted back, pure vitriol in her voice.

The door of the takeaway slammed shut, causing the bell to ring for a good ten seconds longer than usual. Bao helped herself to three pounds and twenty pence from the coins on the counter, before rounding the rest up and handing them to Eddie.

"Your change?" Bao said.

A dumbfounded Eddie took the change and the bag from the counter and rubbed his back with his free hand. He turned to Rob, who looked as puzzled as he was shocked.

"Wow," Rob said. "I wouldn't want to mess with her."

"She's a sweetheart really," Eddie said, sounding like he was one bad thought away from crying.

"You can still get her, mate. Take the food and the change and find her."

"Nah. She's out of my league anyway. I'll just go back to mine and eat this. It's better to have loved and lost, ey?"

"Looks to me like you had a lucky escape, mate. She's a little aggressive."

The two men shared a quiet, reflective moment.

"I like you, Rob," Eddie said. "You're a dead nice chap."

"You're a good lad, Eddie. You'll find someone else in time."

"Nah. I think she's the one. Maybe I'm doomed to walk the earth alone, or at least until I grow up a little and sort my shit out?" Eddie said, thoughtfully.

"Maybe you're right, mate. Sorting that quick temper out might be a start."

"Yeah, I do get a bit aggressive. Especially when I'm hungry."

Rob was quite taken with this scruffy little romantic.

"Good night, Rob. Enjoy your grub," Eddie said. He looked at his bag of food and sighed. "I'm going to have a good long think about what you've said. I can't go around being stupid and angry all the time. It's time I grew up."

Rob nodded in agreement, and Eddie stepped up to the door. He opened it just enough for it to connect to the bell, and then stopped. Rob glanced over as Eddie bowed his head and his grip on the door handle tightened. In a split second, Eddie's vision of a naked Katie lying on his bed clouded any thoughts of maturity, and his anger overcame him once again.

"CAT FUCKERS!!" Eddie screamed, and he used his head start to launch himself across the street and away before Shun could come out and catch him.

Rob leapt out of his seat and watched from the door as Shun gave chase down the street, dressed in a white apron and matching hat, holding his meat cleaver. His hat fell off as he sprinted after Eddie.

Shun turned and cursed Eddie as he made his way back to his kitchen via the back door, and Rob decided it would be wise to sit down and shut up until the food was ready. He didn't want his association with Eddie to result in a 'special' sauce.

After a few minutes, Rob's heart rate reached normal levels, and he thought about what Eddie had said to him regarding his expectations as to what Rob would be like. He considered himself a big softy, but the more he thought about it, the more he realised that what Faye had said to him was true. Like a town-wide game of Chinese whispers, Rob's 'legend' had grown over time, and it was time he stopped feeding the storytellers.

Rob devised a set of rules in his head, and he was looking forward to telling Faye about them. Number one was 'No more goat', and number two was 'Sunday lunch instead of Saturday night'. Two simple changes that would dramatically reduce the risk of having to punch somebody in the face.

Rob's wish-fulfilment daydream was broken by the sound of the telephone ringing, and Bao appeared holding Rob's food at the same time. They shared a smile, and Rob gestured for Bao to answer the phone first. Bao nodded her appreciation and answered the phone, grabbing her book of post-it notes and Argos pen. "Hello. Huh-huh... Huh-huh... I read back... One... Sixteen... Twenty-nine... Six... Six... Forty-two... Huh-Huh... Huh-Huh... Fifteen minutes. Bye."

Rob paid for his food and left The Golden Fleece with a bag that smelled delicious. He sent a text message to Faye with his free hand, writing: 'I survived! On my way home. Love you lots', and put his phone back in his jacket.

11

The darkened street leading out of the town was deserted, and the streetlights reflecting on the rain soaked pathways looked like an oil slick. All that could be heard was the distant sound of singing, coming from the lungs of Andy as he tottered back and forth from the road to the safety of the path in a drunken stupor.

"White men sing, only fools Shaolin," he sang, with as much tone and clarity as a throttled animal.

Ben swayed from side-to-side and swung on a lamp post.

"I love a bit of WD-40," he said.

"How dare you!" Andy said, attempting to stand still and failing. "It's Elvis Presley. And it's UB40. WD-40 is a lubricant, knob breath."

"Either way, you can't sing for shit."

Andy ignored him and moved on to butchering Scorpions.

"Follow the Boss-Wah, down to Donkey Park. Listening to the wind, of chaaaaaaaaaaaange!"

Ben tottered over to a wall and urinated against it, breaking Andy out of his power ballad. He looked over his shoulder to make sure his friend had stopped for him.

"I do like our drunk walks home. You're almost always guaranteed to get into an adventure," Andy said, grinning like a fool.

"Yeah! Do you remember when we stole those 'For Sale' signs and put them outside different people's houses?" Ben said.

"That was funny. I'd have loved to have seen the owners' face when he came out in his bathrobe the next morning to grab his milk and newspaper."

"'Doris, are we moving house?'" Ben said.

They burst into laughter.

"Longest. Piss. Ever," Andy said, growing impatient.

"I can never write my name in piss," Ben murmured.

"What?" Andy asked.

"I was just muttering to myself."

Ben put his tackle away and rejoined his friend, who quickly pointed out something on his jeans.

"You've double-dribbled," he said.

Ben looked down, spotting the small stain on his jeans and shrugging his shoulders.

"Accidents happen. You shouldn't be looking at my goolies anyway."

"It's hard not to see your piss-stained pants when it takes up half your trouser leg."

Ben shook his head, as if he was attempting to shake off the indignity of the situation.

"Can I tell you something?" he asked, a sudden sobering in his voice.

"Of course, you're my best friend," Andy said, grinning and attempting to walk straight.

"I think I fancy the girl from the kebab shop."

"Ahh, *that's* why you didn't want to queue for food?"

"No. I didn't want to queue for food because I was desperate for a piss."

"Uh-huh," Andy said, losing interest fast.

"I've never been in there sober, and she's really quiet. I don't want her to get to know me at my worst."

"What are you saying? You want to ask her out?" Andy asked.

"Yeah. But I'm afraid. She's heard me say horrendous things when I'm drunk. She's bound to say no. She won't see that I'm a sensitive soul underneath."

"Underneath your piss-pants," Andy deadpanned.

Ben sighed.

"I was only joking," Andy said, realising that his friend was serious. "You are a lovely guy, Ben. I love you."

"Do you?" Ben perked up instantly.

"Of course I do. You're my best friend. She'd be lucky to have you."

"Thanks mate."

Andy stopped still and opened his arms out.

"Gizza hug," he said.

"Do you really want to hold me in the rain?"

"Yup," Andy said, willing him in with his open palms.

Ben fell into Andy's embrace, and he closed his eyes as Andy's warm arms held him close.

"I love you, too," Ben said.

Andy rubbed his friend's back as he held him tightly.

"You'll find a nice girl one day, mate. We both will. Probably when we stop wanting to drink beer so much. Until then, we'll have to make do with each other."

Ben nodded in agreement.

Andy looked up to see the lights of The Golden Fleece were still on at the end of the road.

"Do you fancy some chicken balls? My treat?" he asked.

"Yeah, go on then," Ben replied, his voice muffled from planting his face in Andy's shoulder.

The two friends broke away from the embrace and made their way to the Chinese takeaway. As they approached, they saw Eddie Howard run for his life across the street.

"Little bastard," Andy said.

From behind the pair, a wooden gate flung open, and Shun ran out after Eddie in his apron, carrying a meat cleaver. Andy and Ben jumped out of their skins, and watched as Shun gave chase, only to give up at the end of the road. They were rooted to the spot as Shun made his way back.

"You'll never catch him," Ben said, attempting to make Shun feel better. "The stinky little shitbag stole my bike three years ago and I've never been able to catch him. He's got lightning in those legs."

Shun stopped at the gate and stared at the two men for a moment.

"Fuck you!" he said, and slammed the gate shut.

Andy and Ben turned to each other, shocked.

"How rude," Andy said.

"I don't think we should get any of Shun's balls tonight," Ben said.

"That's a T-shirt," Andy said. The joke passed right over Ben's head.

As they approached The Fleece, the aromas hit their nostrils, and the doubt started to creep in.

"On second thoughts, I am quite hungry," Andy said, his will bending by the second.

"Is it *Jason and The Argonauts* with the golden fleece in it?" Ben asked, looking up at the sign.

"Nah, I think that was *Clash of The Titans*."

"I'm pretty sure it was *Jason*. It's definitely one of those Greek films with plasticine models in it."

"That's not plasticine. Plasticine is what Tony Hart used for Morph."

The pair stopped talking and looked at each other for a moment.

"What the fuck are we talking about?" Andy asked, as much to himself as Ben.

Before they could answer their rhetorical question, Rob left the takeaway holding a bag of food, and Ben suddenly remembered that they'd left the pub to find Rob and watch him in a brawl.

"There's Rob! There's Rob!" he cried out.

"Where?" Andy said, still staring at The Golden Fleece's sign. Ben pointed to him.

"There, dickhead. You and your clashes of fucking titans. We left the pub to find Rob and watch him flip those cockneys!"

The pair ran pathetically after Rob, and their shoes clumped against the pavement as they resembled a couple of ponies wearing fresh hooves. They were panting after ten seconds of running. Rob spun around, then relaxed when he saw that it was those dopey fools and not someone looking for a fight.

"Rob! Rob! How's it going?" Andy asked, gasping for air.

"Not bad. Unlike you two. Have you been in the pub all night?" Rob asked.

"All day."

"Ah, that explains it. The Goat?" he asked.

"Nah, The Bull," Ben said.

"Ah right. I would've seen you in The Goat."

"You've been in there tonight?" Andy asked.

"Just for a couple. I got fed up and wanted to have a late supper with the missus, y'know?"

"Good idea, mate," Ben said.

He looked at Andy, who shared his relief. The idea of a fight sounded much more interesting when they weren't drenched, hungry and hadn't just shared a man hug in the rain. They were happy to see Rob out of trouble and heading home, but then the smell from Rob's bag hit their noses. They looked down at it like a couple of vultures.

"Whatcha got there, buddy?" Andy asked.

"Just a few bits and bobs. Chow Mein, chicken balls, spare ribs and egg fried rice," he said.

"We were desperate for a naan sandwich but the queue was too long," Ben said, staring at the bag like a man possessed.

"Yeah, they're a bit slow in the Turkish place, aren't they?" Rob asked, sympathetically. "The girl in there's cute, though. Natasha, isn't it?"

"Yup, and Ben's in love with her," Andy said.

"No I'm not!" Ben snapped.

Rob felt like he had interrupted a domestic dispute. He took a step back, hoping that this would prompt Andy and Ben to say their farewells so he could leave for home without feeling rude.

"I'll leave you to it, lads," he said.

"That sure smells nice, Rob. Did you get free prawn crackers as well?" Ben asked.

"Yes I did."

"They're good 'uns in there, aren't they?" Andy said, before finally asking the question that was on both his and Ben's lips. "Give us a whiff of the bag, Rob."

They resembled a pair of wolves closing in on a wounded animal.

"Err, no. Sorry lads. Why not just go in there and order something yourself?" he asked.

"I think we've annoyed Shun. Right now he's stirring the sweet and sour sauce with his willy, waiting for us to come in and order."

"Well you can't piss him off any more than Eddie Howard has. He called him a cat fucker and got chased down the street," Rob said.

"That seems to be a reoccurring problem for Shun," Ben said.

"News travels fast. There does seem to be a shortage of cats around here," said Andy.

"They're all at home snuggled up by the fire," said Rob. "Only fools like us come out in this cold. And on that bombshell, I bid you both a fond farewell."

Rob picked his sweet and sour chicken balls out of the bag and teased the starving drunks with it, passing it under their noses and grinning like a Cheshire cat. Andy and Ben stood with open mouths like obedient dogs, and Rob burst out laughing.

"You look like something out of a Tom and Jerry cartoon," he said. "Sorry for being a bastard, but it had to be done. See ya later."

Rob put the food back in the bag and turned to leave, but then something caught his attention out of the corner of his eye. Two men were standing in the shadows across the road. The streetlight was reflecting off a metal frame that one of the figures was wearing, causing Rob to stop dead in his tracks and try and work out what it was.

Seconds later, a huge bang ricocheted through the air. It was too loud to be a firework, and the fact that something blasted Rob's bag of food clean out of his hand at the same time all but confirmed it.

Andy dropped to the floor, and Ben dived on top of him.

"It's a fucking drive-by!" Ben screamed.

Rob stood deadly still. The shock had paralysed him, and his ears were ringing like Big Ben had chimed next to his head. He stared across the street, panting in shock, and soon enough, Ray and Clive walked into view.

Clive's headgear was shimmering in the streetlight, and Ray was holding what appeared to be an antique shotgun. Rob gasped for air as the two approached, with Ray charging forward with murderous intent. He raised the weapon, and Rob closed his eyes as he had seen enough films to know that shotguns could fire two shells.

Time to go, he thought. He pictured Liam dressed in a suit, staring solemnly at the grassy ground of a cemetery. His mother's hands resting on his shoulders.

Click.

That shot is going to kill me at any second, he thought. He pictured Liam at his graduation, with a greying Faye championing her boy. All grown up. A man.

Click. Click.

I'm still alive, he thought. Fuck these clichés. Click. Click. Click.

Rob opened his eyes. Ray was standing at the curb, pointing the shotgun right at his chest. His face was a mixture of confusion and terror; his tools had let him down at the pivotal moment. There was only one way that Rob was going to react now that it had come down to bare knuckles.

Rob shook the sound of ringing from his ears and opened his eyes as wide as he could to stretch himself back to full focus. The ringing stopped. The focus returned. The fists clenched.

"Hurry ush! Hurry ush!" Clive slurred through his headgear, his panic and the combination of alcohol and meds. Ray turned to his associate and yelled:

"Shut up you twa—"

Before Ray could finish his sentence, he was sparked out by a right hook, served perfectly to the chin by Rob. His body went limp as it connected, folding him like a deckchair and leaving him sprawled out on his back. The shotgun fell to the ground, and Rob kicked it over to Andy and Ben, before dragging Ray out of the road and lifting him onto the pavement so that he wouldn't be a sitting duck for the next car that turned the corner. He put him into the recovery position and marched over to Andy and Ben.

Andy pushed Ben off him and picked up the shotgun. He couldn't quite believe it was real as he examined it. Ben dragged himself to his feet, and glanced over to the unconscious Ray. For some strange reason, he seemed devastated.

"Did we miss it again?" he asked.

"What?" Andy asked, stroking the shotgun as he studied every part of it.

"The somerflip!" Ben said, on the verge of tears.

Andy shrugged his shoulders. He had a shotgun now. He didn't need to know whether or not Ray had done a 360 degree flip from a punch.

"How are you holding up, guys?" Rob asked, placing a reassuring hand on Andy's shoulder.

"Did he flip, Rob?" Ben asked.

"What?" Rob asked.

"Did he flip?"

"Did that blast burst an eardrum or something?" Rob asked, confused to the point of becoming angry. "Of course he didn't flip, you idiot. What's that got to do with anything?"

"The guy from *Hellraiser* over there," Ben said, and pointed over to Clive, who was standing in the road and shaking like a leaf. "That's the guy you somerflipped a while back. Remember?"

Rob turned to Clive and tried to remember him.

Andy's obsession with the gun was distracted by Rob's hand, which seemed to be covered in blood. He called out to Rob as he approached Clive, whose trembling increased with every step Rob took closer.

"Your hand's bleeding," Andy said.

"It's sauce," Rob said.

That was good enough for Andy, and he went back to playing with his new toy.

Rob stopped in front of Clive, who had wet himself in all of the commotion. He put his hands up to protect himself, and Rob frowned at him.

"Do you think I'd punch someone in the condition you're in?" he said. "Do you think I'm a bloody savage?"

"No," Clive whimpered.

"That's the second time you've ruined my dinner. It's the last as well. Do you understand?"

"Yessh. I promish."

"Good," Rob said. He turned to Andy and Ben. "Are you two sober enough to stay here and watch these two? I'll call the police and get home. My wife's expecting me."

The notion of being asked by Rob to do anything was enough to make Andy and Ben stand up straight and act as soberly and earnest as they had all night.

"Absolutely, Rob!" said Ben.

"You can count on us!" said Andy, swinging the shotgun like a cricket bat.

Rob wasn't filled with confidence, but he didn't have much choice but to trust them. He wanted to get the hell away from the scene.

"I was sobering up anyway," Ben said, in an attempt to reassure Rob. "Hardly touched a drop."

Rob shook his head in bemusement, but it was good enough for him. He turned to Clive and looked him right in the eye.

"You got off lightly. If you weren't wearing that thing on your head, you'd be snoring like your friend. I want you to take this opportunity to think about what you're doing, then fuck off and never come back. I never want to see you again. The next time I do, I'll stick that shotgun up your arse. Understood?"

Clive winced, then nodded.

"Undershtood," he said.

"Enjoy your police cell," Rob said, before turning and nodding to Andy and Ben. He grabbed his steaming bag of food, shrugged his shoulders, and jogged off down the street. Andy and Ben looked like a couple of lovesick girls watching Superman leaving a crime scene.

"How fucking cool is Rob?" Ben said.

"I think he likes us," Andy said.

"Definitely."

"Imagine how cool we're going to sound now? 'Oh yeah, some guy shot at Rob, but we saved him and helped him get home to his missus'."

Andy was a little thrown back by Ben's version of events.

"That's not really what happened, mate."

"And? Chinese whispers, innit?"

Andy nodded along.

"I get it now," he said, then turned and pointed to the sign above the door of The Golden Fleece. "*And* it happened outside a Chinese."

"I'm telling you, we're going to be legends after this. Nobody's going to mess with us again after they find out what happened here."

"I know. And I've still got the shotgun as proof," Andy said.

"You should probably hide that. Or give it to the police."

"Yeah, maybe. Oh wait!"

Andy jigged on the spot like a happy child. He had an idea. He ran to the curb and placed his foot on Ray, who was still unconscious, and posed with the shotgun in the air, like a big game hunter showing off his prize.

"Take a picture!" Andy said.

"You look like He-Man!" Ben said, barely able to contain his excitement as he rummaged through his pockets for his phone. He found it, and prepared to take a picture.

"I HAVE THE POWER!"

Andy's voice boomed out, only for it to be silenced when the shotgun found itself unjammed and went off, causing Andy to relieve himself in his jeans and collapse in a heap next to Ray.

Ben fell back into the wall in shock, before bursting into hysterical laughter as he spotted his friend's wet patch.

"Hey look!" he said, pointing at Clive and Andy's similar problem. "You two look like brothers with your piss-stained pants!"

"Ha-ha, very funny. Don't forget that you were the first one to forget your potty training tonight," Andy said, dragging himself upright and trying hard not to have a heart attack.

Ben's face dropped. He didn't take kindly to being caught out when he was telling jokes at someone else's expense. Before he could retaliate, the distant sound of police sirens could be heard.

"Behave now, the police are on the way," Ben said.

"They're probably on their way to The Goat to pull a pint glass out of somebody's face. Shall we ring them ourselves, or do you think someone else will? I don't want to ring them. I hate cops."

"And they're not fans of us, either."

"That's what I mean. They'll see all of us standing here with piss pants and arrest us all for public indecency."

"*Exactly* what I was thinking," Ben said.

The two stopped talking and shuffled around on the spot. Clive stood and watched them, unsure of whether to make a run for it or burst into tears. He chose to do the latter, and the whimpering soon caught the attention of Andy and Ben.

"Now, now, now. Don't cry. What's wrong with you?" Ben asked.

"I've entered the seventh circle of hell! That's what's wrong with me!" Clive yelled.

"You just spoke properly!" Andy observed.

"It's hard to feel any pain in your jaw when you're whole body has been thrown into shock. My life flashed before my eyes!"

Andy was momentarily distracted by Ray's murmuring as he woke from his punch-induced snooze. He stepped up to him and booted him on the chin, knocking him clean out again.

"I think the same thing just happened to him," Andy said, turning to Clive. "Only his life looked surprising like a big toe."

Ben laughed, and high-fived his friend as he limped past.

"What's up with you?" he asked.

"I think I just took my toenail off with that kick," Andy said, wincing. "It hurts like a bastard and I can feel a squelch in my sock."

"Like he's got a squelch in his pants?" Ben said, nodding over to a sobbing Clive.

"Yeah!" Andy giggled, albeit whilst limping. "Thanks for making me laugh, Ben. It's taking my mind off my toe."

"Bless you. You're welcome, mate. Although that toe is going to hurt once the alcohol wears off."

"Don't remind me about my toe!" Andy shrieked.

The police sirens became louder.

"Yup, somebody called the cops. Typical," Ben said, shaking his head in disappointment.

"Thank fucking Christ!" Clive yelped.

Andy and Ben turned to each other, then back to Clive.

"You're getting boring now, climbing frame face!" Andy said, and the two men started to approach him. Ben cracked the knuckles on both hands as the two closed in on their whimpering foe.

"C'mon, fellas. Your mate wouldn't want you to hurt me. Look at my face!" Clive pleaded.

"Who said we have to hit you in the face?" Ben said, bluntly, and threw a left hook that connected with Clive's ribcage. It took all the puff out of his lungs, and he dropped to the floor in pain. Andy and Ben carried on sticking the boot in, until Ben jumped back onto the pavement and screamed.

"Bastard!" he yelled.

"What's up with you now?" Andy asked, as Clive crawled up to Ray and lay on him.

"I think I've taken my toenail off as well," said Ben.

"How alike are we?" Andy said, smiling like it was something to be proud of.

"Toe-tally," Ben said, and waited for Andy to get the joke.

"Brilliant! A toe-tal triumph!" Andy continued the run.

"I'm going tee-toe-tal after tonight."

"From now on, you shall be known as, McBrokentoe!"

Name calling was one step too far for Ben.

"Don't start on my deformities now!" he said.

The red and blue flashing lights couldn't come quick enough for Clive, who huddled up to Ray and waited for the police to arrive, praying that Andy and Ben were as stupid as they looked, and would keep themselves distracted long enough to stop kicking him.

12

It was a little past 10pm, and Faye was sitting on the sofa in a thick-fleeced pink dressing gown, thinking of ways to get Rob to open up. She had devised a couple of ideas, and one of them involved getting all of the photo albums out onto the dining room table, so that they could go through them. She hoped that this would evoke some kind of emotional reaction, just like Maggie had told her it would.

Faye had made sure the albums that included the most photos of Ken were on top; so that Liam would ask questions and Rob would have to find answers for them. Nothing brings the truth out of you better than the brutal honesty of a child. Faye felt a little guilty for using manipulative tactics, but she also knew that it was essential to her feeling more comfortable when Liam was in the playground, the classroom and later in his life.

Faye's other idea was to talk to Rob while he was drunk. Unless there'd been an incident while he was out, Rob was a pleasant and amusing drunk. Faye likened him to one the goons from *Popeye*, which would prompt him to do an impression, including throwing Faye onto his shoulder like she was Olive Oyl.

Faye flitted between watching TV and playing games on her phone as she waited for Rob to come home. When Rob burst through the front door with the force of a wrecking ball, she expected him to be blind drunk. Instead, he staggered into the living room like a man possessed. His eyes were wild and he was more pale than usual, and Faye saw fear in him for the first time ever.

"Oh my God, what happened to you?" she asked, moving so that Rob could collapse onto the sofa. Rob was holding a bag of Chinese food with a gigantic hole in the middle, and he was clinging to the bag for dear life.

"The boy... Where's the boy?" Rob asked, panicking.

"In bed, where you left him," Faye replied, stroking his hair to help calm him down.

"Has anybody been round? Anybody called?"

"No. Why? What happened?" Faye lifted Rob's chin so that she could see his eyes. "Are you on crack or something? Nobody's been here since you left."

"I've really messed up this time," he said.

Faye instantly thought the worst. She pictured Rob hitting someone and them slipping into a coma. She saw flashing ambulance lights and the crunching sound of handcuffs as they tightened around his wrists as the police led him away.

"Tell me what happened. I can't help you if you don't tell me," she said, softly.

"I had a gun fired at me," Rob paused, then snorted as he laughed at the ridiculousness of what had just come out of his mouth. "Imagine that? A gun. Fired at me. What the fuck?"

Faye couldn't speak. She stepped away from Rob, colour fading from her face with every step she took. Seeing her like this straightened Rob up a little more quickly.

"What do you mean, 'I had a gun fired at me'?" she asked. "Who fired a gun at you, Rob?"

The panic started to creep into Faye's bones, and those thoughts of Rob hurting somebody turned into visions of armed men coming to the house where Liam slept upstairs.

"I'm waiting for the punchline," she said, as much to herself as Rob.

Rob suddenly bolted across the room to the large windows. He opened the curtains and looked out into the street. They were empty except for streetlights, rain and the shadows of the neighbouring trees.

"Rob, I need to know what's going on," Faye said. "Are we in danger? Is Liam in danger?"

The use of Liam's name spun Rob's attention away from the streets back to Faye.

"I'd never let anybody hurt Liam. That's why I ran home," he said.

"Tell me what's going on then!" Faye said, at the edge of her wits.

Rob grabbed Faye's arm and sat her down next to him on the sofa.

"A few weeks back, I was walking home when this Londoner starts having a go at me. He was calling me a townie and getting in my face, and then he knocked my food out of my hand. I punched him and knocked him out."

Faye bowed her head in disappointment.

"Why?" she asked.

"Because that's what you do when a guy gets in your face and acts like a bloody fool, Faye."

"No, it's what *you* do when a guy acts like a bloody fool, which makes you more of one, because you have a child and you should know better."

Rob was in no mood to be lectured. He stood up and paced back and forth. Faye couldn't bring herself to look at him.

"So what happened?" she asked, more angry than concerned.

"He came back from London today, with a friend who had a gun."

"And?"

"And they approached me outside of The Golden Fleece and shot at me. The first shot hit this bag. I brought it back for evidence... and in case you were hungry."

"Hungry?" Faye said, a nervous laugh coming out at Rob's stupidity. "You think I want to eat after hearing about you nearly being killed?"

"I'm OK. The shotgun was an antique, only good for one shot at a time. It jammed before he could try again so I took my opportunity and sparked him out."

"What did his friend do? The last one you 'sparked out'," Faye asked.

"He just stood there and pissed himself."

Faye put her head into her hands and sighed. Rob took her hands in his.

"It's going to be alright," he said, reassuringly.

"You've got to be more careful. You shouldn't knock out people from London."

"What difference does it make where they're from?" Rob said.

"London is a dangerous place."

"*This* is a dangerous place! I just got my sweet and sour chicken fired out of my hand by a shotgun!"

"Don't talk about this like it's a joke. You could've been killed."

Faye looked down at Rob's reddened hand.

"Oh my God, you're hurt," she said.

"It's a sauce burn."

Faye allowed herself a laugh, but it was in despair as much as anything else.

"We're going to have to move," she said. "They might come back with reinforcements. It'll never end. It's like those black gangster movies with Ice Cubes in it."

"What are you talking about?" Rob asked, confused.

"The one with the drive-by and the 'Show me the money' guy."

"*Boyz 'N' The Hood*?" Rob said, still trying to figure out where the conversation was heading.

"Exactly. Are we going to be in trouble?" she asked.

"No. I'm pretty sure it's over now," Rob said, stroking her hands.

"How can you be so sure?"

"I left them both with Andy and Ben. They were passing and offered to stand watch until the police arrived."

The words 'Andy' and 'Ben' were enough to increase Faye's heart beats per minute by seventy-five percent.

"That doesn't fill me with confidence," Faye said. "I wouldn't trust them to babysit a hamster, let alone two armed and dangerous Londoners."

"Don't worry, Andy has the gun, and like I said, it was jammed."

"This gets worse!" Faye said. "Andy used to eat ink cartridges at school. He once put a metal ruler under a Bunsen burner and put it on Ben's neck as a joke. He's probably blown his face off by now."

Rob laughed.

"They'll be fine. I called the police on the way home. I needed to get out of there and back to you."

"If you're so sure that they'd be fine, why were you so paranoid and afraid when you first came in?" Faye asked.

Rob paused for a moment. The words he wanted to say didn't come naturally to him. As far as he was concerned, they didn't belong in his vocabulary.

"Because I was in shock," he said, before pausing again. "And afraid."

Faye grabbed his face and forced him to look at her.

"You've got no reason to be ashamed of that. Of course you were afraid."

"Who's afraid?" a voice asked from the doorway. Faye and Rob's eyes shot to the door, where Liam was standing in his pyjamas, rubbing his eyes and yawning.

Rob held out his arms, and Liam ran and dived into them. He held him more tightly than he ever had before, and urged Faye to huddle in and do the same. She obliged.

"What's wrong?" Liam asked. "I could hear you talking."

"I had a nightmare," Rob said, spitting out the first excuse that came into his head.

"What about?" Liam asked.

"That I lost you and your mum."

Liam laughed.

"You silly old fool. It was only a dream. Nothing to get upset about. We're not going anywhere, are we, Mum?"

Faye shook her head.

"I know, buddy. I think I had some dodgy chicken," Rob said.

"It's cheese that gives you nightmares," Liam said.

"Know-it-all!"

Rob wrestled and tickled Liam into a frenzy, but was quickly interrupted by the doorbell. A deathly silence fell on the room, as Faye and Rob froze and Liam looked at them in confusion.

"It's just the doorbell," Liam said.

Rob and Faye moved over to the window. Faye peered through a gap in the curtains, but couldn't see anyone at the door.

"Do you think they've come back to finish you off?" Faye whispered.

Rob shook his head, but still whispered, just in case.

"If they have, they're awfully polite to ring the doorbell first," he said. "And we're cancelling Sky, by the way. No more gangster films for you."

The doorbell rang again.

"Why are you whispering and acting weird?" Liam asked.

Rob turned to Liam, who was looking at his parents like they'd gone mad. It threw him out of his overprotective mode. He approached the front door and opened it until the safety chain kicked in.

"Hello?" he said, making sure his head wasn't in full view. Just in case.

"Hello," a friendly, gruff-sounding male voice came from the other side. "It's Sergeant Henry. Can I have a word?"

Rob recognised the voice immediately, and his posture changed. A weight had been lifted, and he took the chain off the door and opened it.

"Good evening," Rob said.

"It was," the Sergeant replied.

Sergeant Henry was well known around the town for being the main authority in the town's police force. He was in his late fifties, had a bushy grey beard, and resembled David Bellamy, if he'd become a police officer instead of a botanist.

The Sergeant was especially good at dealing with the disenfranchised youth of the town. Whereas some of the other police officers in the town treated the scallies like a boil on the arse, Henry would refer to them by their surnames – Mr Thomas, for example – and get to know them: their interests, their hopes, strengths and weaknesses, and try to steer them back to the right path. The kids would often refer to him as 'the lesser bastard', which to Henry was as close to a compliment as he was likely to get.

Suffice to say, Henry had known Rob for a long time, and his father before him, and he'd seen all manner of events take place in the town. But on this night, even he was experiencing a first.

Liam appeared, and looked up at the burly bearded man standing outside in full uniform.

"Is my daddy in trouble?" he asked.

"No, son. But I will be soon if he doesn't let me get out of the rain," Henry joked.

Rob moved away from the door and allowed Henry to enter. The Sergeant brushed himself down and took off his shoes.

"Go in and sit down. I'll make us a drink," Rob said.

"No trouble, no trouble," Henry said.

"OK. In that case, after you."

Sergeant Henry entered the living room, where Faye was standing.

"Good evening, my dear," he said.

"Good evening," Faye said, unsure of what to do with herself. "Can I get you anything?"

"Rob's just asked me, love. I'm fine thanks. I do need to speak to him alone though, if you don't mind?"

Faye nodded, put her hands on Liam's shoulders and ushered him out of the room. As soon as they left, Sergeant Henry loosened his act a little, becoming much more informal. He bent down and picked up the Chinese takeaway bag. He held it up, looking through the hole and into the light from the ceiling shining through. He chuckled to himself and put the bag down.

"You lucky, lucky, lucky bastard," Henry said. "The Chinese gods must be smiling down on you, Robbo."

"Yeah?" Rob asked rhetorically. "Couldn't this have waited until the morning? I've been shot at and I'm starving."

"You don't have to play the big man with me, Rob. The tears haven't long dried on those cheeks," Henry said.

Rob looked up at the Sergeant, who was smiling at him.

"I wanted to let you know that we've arrested the two Londoners."

"Thank you."

"There's two of my guys at the station acting out scenes from *Get Carter* with the shotgun found at the scene. I've never seen them looking so happy, bless 'em."

"Lovely," Rob said.

"We picked up a drunk lad who was walking down the high street naked, singing that 'Scatman John' song. We brought him in the station and when he saw us pissing about with the gun, he begged us to let him re-enact the scene where Michael Caine walks the guy into the street at gunpoint, nuts swinging in the wind. That would have been unprofessional though."

Rob looked at Sergeant Henry and wondered what he had been smoking.

"Great film, great film," Henry said, still enjoying his daydream. He shook his head and refocused. "Sorry, where was I?"

"I'm glad my near-death experience has brought so much joy to the town and its police force," Rob deadpanned.

"Oh it has! I had to arrest Andy and Ben as well though. Not the cleverest idea to give them any responsibility. I wouldn't trust them to open a bottle of wine with a screw top."

"I didn't have much choice. There weren't many people around, and I wanted to get back here."

"Makes sense, makes sense. They'd kicked the living shit out of those cockneys when we'd got there, and then Ben called the owner of the Chinese a cat fucker when he came out to inspect the noise. I had to pry a meat cleaver out of his hand. Ben was crying like a baby. Pissed his pants. All of them had, strangely..."

"I was really scared, you know," Rob said, cutting Sergeant Henry off.

Henry shook his head.

"I don't doubt it at all. I was merely trying to make light of the situation. I guess it's still early days. I apologise. At least you're back here with your family now. That's the main thing," he said.

Rob stared into space as he remembered being approached by the gunman.

"That Londoner looked right into my eyes and pulled the trigger a hundred times. He would've blown my heart out of my chest without a second's hesitation."

"Just as well he was carrying a weapon that wasn't much cop," Henry said.

Rob glared at Henry, who could see that he was genuinely afraid for his life.

"Who could shoot a man with a wife and a kid without blinking an eye? What world are we living in?"

Henry sat down in the single chair next to the sofa and exhaled. He wasn't used to being the one being asked the question.

"You're asking the wrong man, Rob," he sighed. "Why do people do anything? I don't have an answer. Last week a kid tried to hang himself after being hounded on Facebook for months about being gay. The poor lad's in a coma, and his parents said that he's been getting more abuse than ever before. If I tried to make sense of these things, I think I'd have retired a long time ago."

The two men shared a silence as both their stories sunk in.

"If I hadn't been able to grab that shotgun and knock him out…" Rob trailed off before he could finish the sentence.

"Thank your lucky stars he was a lousy shot, too," Henry said. He looked down at the bag of food. "It doesn't look like the egg fried rice survived the ordeal."

Henry picked up the bag and examined it again.

"And your spare ribs are fucked!"

"I'll get over it. So what happens now?" Rob asked.

"I'll need to get a statement," Henry said, snapping back into duty mode. "Andy and Ben's tale won't stand up in court because they were drunk. And because they're Andy and Ben. This is more of a courtesy call. I wanted to make sure you're alright."

"My heart feels like it's had a cocaine injection. I'm sure I'll live though."

"I think it might be a good idea to get out of the firing line for a while. No pun intended," Henry chuckled.

"And how do you suppose I do that, Henry? My reputation stands for itself, and those who don't know me just want to fight the big fella."

"Just stay out of the pubs that are frequented by dickheads. I know that's difficult, especially in this town, but give it a shot. Maybe spend a bit more time with your son? Get involved in what he's interested in."

"I already do," Rob shot back. "I'm not a thug, you know?"

"I know that. You're just an easy target. You're someone for the muppets of this town to gauge their toughness on."

"It's the way it's always been, and it will be as long as I'm here. Liam'll be fighting my name in years to come, but he's cut from a different cloth," Rob said.

"At least you're aware of it. You can do everything in your power to prevent it. Starting now. Some people love to pass on their hard man reputation through the generations. Your dad basked in this kind of limelight, but I know you don't want it."

"One hundred percent."

"Plus, it's only a matter of time before you take someone's head clean off with one of those punches," Henry said, smiling. "You should've been a boxer. Who's heavyweight champion these days?"

"Klitschko?" Rob said, not totally sure.

"That's the one. I haven't followed it since Tyson dined out on Holyfield... What was the point I was making?"

"I should knock out Ukrainians?"

"Yeah... No! I mean you should've been a boxer. Put that skill to good use."

"I wouldn't have had the discipline. And I like the taste of beer too much," Rob said.

"You're going to have to curb that for a bit. Maybe that'll help you find the discipline, ey?"

Rob nodded in agreement.

"You're a good bloke, Rob. I don't want you to end up in jail on account of knocking out one of these beered-up morons."

"Thanks for the concern."

Faye and Liam appeared.

"He was getting impatient, and worried about his dad," Faye said.

"You've got nothing to worry about, Mr Thomas," Henry reassured Liam, who ran over to his dad and sat on his knee.

"I'll leave you all to your dinner," Henry said, and winked to Faye to let her know that she had nothing to worry about.

"What's left of it," Faye said.

"I'll see myself out."

Sergeant Henry went to leave, but before he reached the door, Rob called out.

"I'll come down and see you at the station tomorrow," he said. "Statements. Whatever you need. You have my full support."

Henry nodded his thanks to Rob, then turned to Liam.

"He's a good man, your dad," he said.

"He's the best," Liam replied, grinning at his dad and not looking away from him for a second.

"I don't doubt it. You all take care now."

Sergeant Henry left the house. Faye didn't want to ask how everything went in front of Liam. She used the wives' trick of using her eyes to ask questions. Rob nodded back.

"What have you been up to?" Liam asked.

"Ah, y'know. Dodging bullets. The usual."

"Cool."

"I'll tell you all about it."

Faye gave Rob a look as if to say 'no you won't', prompting a smile from her exhausted husband.

"Are you going to start telling me stories every night?" Liam asked.

"Until I run out of them."

"Or I get bored."

Rob laughed.

"Yeah. Or you get bored."

Rob pulled Liam into him, and a tickle for being cheeky soon became a long warm embrace as the memory of the night's events and what he could've lost hit home again.

After watching her two boys for a moment, Faye picked up the bag of food, held it up to the light, and examined it.

"Shall we see if the microwave can salvage these ribs?"

13

Sunday lunch was a window of opportunity for The Bull. While the staff of The Goat were sweeping up broken glass and mopping vomit and urine from the toilet floors, Charlie and Gail were making a killing from traditional Sunday lunches, complete with a choice of meats, Yorkshire puddings the size of a baby's head, and potatoes roasted to perfection in duck fat. A vegetarian's nightmare, but a dream for hungry pub-goers. Charlie would take his position at the bar, whilst Gail and Katie brought out the meals. They were an efficient team, and the pub would be heaving from the hours of 12 to 2.

It was around quarter past two when Andy and Ben arrived, each with one foot in plaster and with a crutch aiding their walk, parading them around to whoever was in the pub like it was something to be proud of. They took their rightful place at the bar, and Charlie tried his hardest to look pleased to see them. He knew that it was not a coincidence to see them at this time. Service had just finished, and like a couple of starved dingoes, they were scavenging for leftovers. Free leftovers, to be exact. A tougher landlord would've kicked them out for their cheek, but Charlie had a soft spot for them, even if he had no idea why.

"I'm loving the new attire, lads," Charlie said as he approached the two men, who were struggling to hoist themselves onto their stools. "If Joe Pesci was here he'd be ripping you a new one."

Charlie chuckled at his own joke. Andy and Ben ignored him and concentrated on their stomachs.

"Place smells gorgeous, Charlie," Andy said.

"I'm starving, me," Ben chimed in.

"Do you have any leftovers, Charlie?" Andy asked.

"There's no meat left, I'm afraid," Charlie said, despite the fact that Gail and Katie were tucking into some in the kitchen behind him, and had already plated some up for him.

"What? No yorkies?" Ben asked, devastated.

"I'll have a look for you, but I don't think so."

Charlie loved to torture the pair of them as much as possible. He figured that he let them get away with murder, so it was only fair that he give a little back. He left for the kitchen, where Gail and Katie were picking at potatoes and meat from the hot plate.

"Hi, Dad," Katie said, with a potato wedged in the side of her mouth.

"Don't speak with your mouth full," he replied, as he grabbed a couple of bowls and filled them with potatoes, threw a Yorkshire pudding on top and then smothered them in thick meat gravy.

"Let me guess, the Twat Twins are here?" Gail asked, rolling her eyes.

"Yes, and they look ridiculous. Come and see," Charlie grinned.

"What have they done?"

"They've got bandages on their feet. One each. It's hilarious. They look like a right pair of tits."

"Even more than usual? This I have to see," Katie said.

She took the bowls out of her father's hands and grabbed two forks on the way back to the bar. Charlie turned to Gail and shrugged his shoulders.

Katie burst through the doors of the bar and dropped the two bowls in front of a salivating Andy and Ben, who looked at them like a couple of starved orphans before popping potatoes into their mouths like they were sweets. Andy hummed his approval as he munched.

"Let's have a look at your feet then, toss pots," Katie said, and flopped herself on the bar to take a look. As her stomach landed on the bar, her legs dangled behind her, and Andy and Ben's eyes shot right to her rump, which was plonked in front of them like they'd just ordered it from the menu. Katie giggled at the plaster casts, but the two lads were too busy admiring her behind to care. That was, until she noticed them looking.

"Oi, perverts. Avert your eyes," she said, and jumped back behind the bar.

"I thought your dad said you'd run out of meat?" Andy joked.

Katie gave them the finger and left for the kitchen.

Andy and Ben high-fived each other and munched on their giant Yorkshires.

Charlie came back into the bar and grabbed two pint glasses.

"What are you drinking, lads?" he said.

"What's the sexiest beer you have?" Ben said.

Charlie chuckled. He'd never heard this one before. He opened up his beer menu on the bar under his patrons' noses and pointed to Haacht Brewery Tongerlo Blond, a pale ale that had won awards.

"This is my favourite," he said.

"Two of those then, Charlie. We're celebrating."

"Celebrating? What are you celebrating? Getting free food or the news that you now qualify for the Paralympics?" Charlie jibed as he fetched the beers.

"You can take the Michael out of us as much as you like today, Charlie. We've stepped up in the world," Ben said, with an air of never-before-seen smugness. Andy nodded along smiling as he soaked up the last of his gravy with his Yorkshire.

"What are you talking about?" Charlie asked, confused. He put the beers down on the bar in front of them. Andy and Ben picked up their handsome bottles, observed the labels, and then tapped them together, before taking a swig.

"Spicy," Ben said, reading the label as he nodded his approval.

"That *is* a sexy beer, Charlie."

Charlie was too weirded out to care about the plaudits for his favourite pale ale.

"Well?" he said, waiting to hear the news worth celebrating.

"Rob Thomas has given us the nod of approval," Andy proclaimed, as if he was expecting Charlie to fall to his knees or open a bottle of champagne at the news.

"What does that mean?" Charlie asked.

"We helped him out last night, Charlie," Ben chimed in. "In a big way, too. I don't think the people of this town are going to be laughing at us quite as much anymore."

"Are you sure it was a nod and not a tic?" Charlie asked.

"Nope. It was a definite nod as if to say 'Thank you for everything, I can't show too much appreciation because I have to get home to my wife and kid. But thank you'."

"'And I will compensate you for the loss of your big toenails'," Andy added.

"That might have been a bit too much," Ben said, the painful memory returning to him. "But we're under his wing now. It's a good place to be."

"You two live on another planet to me," Charlie said.

"Planet 'Under Rob's Wing'. I can think of worse planets to live on. The planet from *Star Trek III: The Search for Spock* to name just one."

Charlie thought that he'd heard it all, but this one was on a new level of stupidity. He leant into both men and checked the whites of their eyes, which made Andy and Ben a little uncomfortable.

"Personal space, Charlie," Ben said, turning away from him.

"I'm checking for signs that the painkillers haven't worn off," Charlie said. "But I'm beginning to think that you're both just stupid."

"Bit harsh," Andy said.

"You didn't listen to one little thing I told you the other night, did you? What good is it being under the wing of a lad who attracts people over from London carrying bloody weapons?"

"You've heard, then?" Ben said, a huge grin appearing on his face.

"A shotgun went off in a small town. They'll be hiring reporters at the local paper tomorrow to keep up with the demand on the story."

"It's weird. I can't remember anything from last night until the gunshot went off. It's amazing how a gunshot can sober you up just like that," Ben observed.

"I wish somebody would fire a gunshot every time I got drunk. I didn't even have a hangover this morning," Andy said, before surpassing himself even further in the realm of stupidity. "I bet somewhere like... Compton! Nobody is drunk. You'd get half way through a pint, and *bang!* 'Ooh I think I'll have some more.' *Bang!* I bet there's more people drunk here than in Compton."

"Interesting theory," Ben nodded.

Charlie was furious. His grip tightened on the bar, and he could have ripped the surface of the bar clean off in his frustration at the two idiots flapping their mouths in front of him.

"That's not an interesting theory at all! It's fucking ridiculous!" he said, desperately trying to keep his voice down despite his anger. "The sad thing about places like Compton is that gunshots going off is commonplace, so if you were getting pissed you wouldn't even acknowledge them. The fact that gunshots go off anywhere in the world, let alone in a bloody market town in the East Midlands, is just awful. You really didn't listen to a word I said?"

Charlie was visibly hurt. As much as Andy and Ben wound him up, he'd hate anything bad to happen to them, and he was well aware that with violent acts, there was always escalation, and retribution. The two Londoners had turned up with a gun because one Londoner had been punched. It didn't take Stephen Hawking to work out that the hatchet wouldn't be buried just because they'd failed. What could be next, a rocket launcher fired at the house? A ninja assassin squad being sent to Rob's workplace? Charlie was beginning to feel like the sanest person in the loony bin, and Ben's response to his question all but confirmed it.

"Of course we listened to what you said, Charlie. We've just forgotten it because it happened before the whole gunshot thingy."

"I told you about Rob's dad, and how people who live their lives in violence end up living off that reputation, and their sons are doomed to live up to it."

Andy and Ben stared at Charlie with blank faces. They couldn't remember a single word. Charlie headed to the coffee machine and made himself an espresso.

"Have I become a caricature?" he muttered to himself as much as the two men. Ben mouthed the word 'caricature'. He had no idea what Charlie was talking about. "Am I just the stupid old man working behind a bar, dishing out advice to people who aren't even listening to him?"

"Don't be so hard on yourself, Charlie," Andy said, polishing off his beer.

Charlie drank his espresso and glanced over to his patrons. They slammed their empty bottles on the bar and licked their lips. A melancholy smile appeared on Charlie's face as he made a conscious decision not to allow himself to be drawn in to the dramas of the town. If people wanted a friendly, cuddly barman they could chat with and then forget the second they walked out into the cold, he would oblige them.

"Oh, who am I trying to kid? Why should I try and pass on my wisdom to the next generation. Two more beers, lads?" he said with a smile, straightening his back as he got back into character.

Andy and Ben cheered as the Charlie they knew and loved returned, and the sourness vacated the room.

"Yes please, Charlie! That's more like it. Back to your sexy Scottish self. Two of those beers, please. One for me, one for McBrokentoe!" Andy said.

Charlie flicked the caps off two bottles of beer and placed them in front of them. Ben looked down at his damaged foot and his bottom lip dropped.

"That name is going to stick," he mumbled sadly to himself.

"It will. It really is brilliant. It's one of the only things I remember about the whole night! And we have matching bandages," Andy said.

"Some people are too easily pleased," Charlie said, as he scooped their cash from the bar and threw it in the till. He moved over to them and leant in to ensure their voices stayed at a reasonable level.

"You haven't given me your side of the story from last night yet," he said.

An excited Ben sat up straight to tell the story.

"Oh yes! Well, we got to The Golden Fleece—"

"Wait a second. Shouldn't I be telling the story?" Andy butted in.

"Why?" Ben asked.

"I've got my English GCSE."

"On a resit!"

"I was expelled the first time round! Anyway it's the going back that counts. It showed character."

Charlie's patience was wearing thin again.

"Can you just tell the story please?" he asked.

After all the offensive posturing, Ben handed Andy the stage.

"Go on then."

Andy nodded his thanks and prepared to tell his version of events.

"We left here and went looking for those geezers, and then we got distracted with food and ended up at The Golden Fleece. Oh, why do they call it The Golden Fleece?"

Charlie was thrown off by the sudden change of direction.

"Err, it was originally a Greek restaurant, but the owner died of a heart attack and the wife sold it to the Chinese couple. They kept the name as a tribute to the owner," he said.

The pair of them went 'ahh' in harmony as one of the town's great mysteries was solved. Charlie gave them a look as if to say 'And?' and Andy shook his head to refocus himself on telling his tale.

"Yeah, anyway. We saw Rob coming out of the Chinese and we stopped him to smell his balls."

Charlie and Ben burst out laughing, much to Andy's disdain.

"Am I telling this story or what?" he asked, angrily. "Giggling like a couple of girls."

"Sorry, Andy, carry on," Charlie said, coughing out his final laugh.

"Thank you. So yeah, we were talking to Rob, when suddenly, out of nowhere, those cockneys ran out and fired a shot at Rob. It hit him right in his Chinese."

Charlie and Ben kept making eye contact with each other and smirked as Andy's hilarious lack of self-awareness kept coming back to haunt him in his retelling of the story.

"The bag flew out of his hand, but before the twat could get another shot off, Rob landed a haymaker that made him do a backflip through the air, and he shouted over to us to help him take care of the other guy, who also had a gun. We beat the shit out of them, and then Rob thanked us and told us to stay and take the glory. We didn't want to see him get in trouble with the police so we said: 'Yeah, Rob. You go home to your wife and kiddy. We'll take care of the bacon'." And that was that, really."

Charlie locked eyes with Andy, but didn't say a word. After a few seconds, Andy's forehead started to become clammy, and his eyes flitted left and right. Charlie knew he was talking absolute bullshit, but he decided that it was worth messing with him anyway.

"That's how it happened was it?" Charlie asked, a look of mischief on his face.

"Yup," Andy replied, still uncomfortable with Charlie's eyeballing tactics.

"What about you?" Charlie asked Ben, looking at him and freeing Andy from his judgemental gaze.

"Yep. Exactly like that. Scout's honour."

Charlie stepped back from the two men and nodded, before serving a couple of customers. The two minutes that it took to serve them must have been hell for Andy and Ben, whose paranoia was settling into their bones and threatened to boil over into a tearful confession.

As soon as the customers paid up and left for their seats, Charlie came back and leant in again.

"It's a very interesting story, your version of events," he said.

"Thanks?" Andy said, with zero confidence in his voice.

"I should probably inform you that, because I'd had those two Londoners in here a while, I've had the police in here this morning. They see me as an important part of the investigation."

Andy and Ben began to shrink in their chairs.

"It's a lovely position to be in. You get to see all kinds of evidence, especially when the lead officer is a good friend of the family."

Ben started to anxiously peel the label from his beer bottle.

"CCTV is a wonderful thing. People think it's a bit intrusive, but I think it's fantastic. I've seen all sorts of things from last night. For example, I saw a couple of dickheads stumbling home, only to stop and give each other a warm embrace in the rain. It was very romantic."

Andy and Ben bowed their heads.

"Then it got really interesting. My police friend showed me the recorded footage from outside The Golden Fleece, so I could identify the two Londoners. It had nothing to do with the two muppets that pissed their pants and jumped around like a couple of girls when the gunshot rang out. Or when one of those two muppets pretended the gun was Excalibur."

"Power Sword," Andy muttered under his breath, correcting Charlie.

Silence.

The invitation to planet 'Under Rob's Wing' was looking more and more like a distant dream all of a sudden. Ben thought about this for a moment, and attempted to salvage a little bit of dignity.

"Anybody else seen this?" he asked.

"Of course not," Charlie said. "And it's only funny because you're sitting here in front of me now, and I'm not identifying the people who shot you whilst your parents are identifying you in the morgue."

Andy sighed and looked up at Charlie.

"When did the footage cut out?" he asked.

"Oh, about the moment the Chinese man grabbed you and threatened you with his meat cleaver. You could virtually smell the tears you were crying."

Ben chortled through his nose.

"But I won't tell anyone, because like I've been trying to tell you, the people who live their lives in violence and who live off that reputation will always have somebody after them, and their sons will be doomed to repeat it. Let me know when you want another beer, fellas."

Charlie left Andy and Ben to stew on that one for a moment. They sat in silence, staring forward at their beer bottles. After a few minutes, Andy opened his mouth.

"I think... in the light of this new evidence, we should keep this story to ourselves. Like Charlie says, it could hurt a lot of people if it became public. Don't you agree?"

Ben nodded in agreement, despite looking like he was about to throw up all over the bar.

"I think you've spoken like a truly wise man," Charlie said.

"I think I'm going to call it a day," Ben said, standing up. "I don't really feel like drinking. Going to go home and iron my clothes for work. And stuff."

Ben, sickened with guilt and embarrassment, collected his belongings and stepped off his stool. He turned to his friend.

"You coming?" he asked.

"Nah, not yet," Andy said.

"OK."

Ben feebly put his hand up to say goodbye to Charlie as he left the pub. Charlie nodded to him, before approaching Andy.

"How come you're staying?" he asked.

"I don't want to be alone," Andy replied, which took Charlie by surprise. It was easy to forget that, underneath the dippy faux-tough-guy exterior, there was a scared young man who had just witnessed a gun attack.

"You stay here as long as you like, friend."

Charlie put a reassuring hand on top of Andy's.

"Was it as terrifying as it looked?" Charlie asked.

"It was the most frightening thing I've ever experienced," he replied.

"Look on the bright side. You're still alive, you've got nine toenails left and Ben pissed his pants in front of you so he'll be in your pocket for the rest of his life."

"Yeah, I guess that's a silver lining."

Charlie grabbed Andy another beer and indicated that there wouldn't be a charge for it. Andy managed an appreciative smile.

"I bet the police pissed themselves when they turned up at the scene and found you two hobbling around," Charlie said, lightening the mood. "What did they say?"

"Not a lot really. I think they've seen weirder things in their time. They were more concerned for the guy with a hamster cage on his head. Which makes sense. They just patched us up and sent us on our way."

"Bloody hell. Did you make statements or anything?"

"Yeah, all that procedural bollocks. Had a nice cup of tea there, too. Bourbons."

"Lovely. What happens now?"

"I don't know, and I don't care. I hope I never have to see those cockney bastards again. I'll probably get called to court though. In about twenty years' time."

Charlie shook his head in disbelief at it all. Something was still troubling Andy though.

"You didn't happen to see if the cockney did a somerflip when Rob smacked him, did you?" Andy asked.

"No, he didn't. In fact, I'm not even sure if it's physically possible. And as Ben is the only one to have seen it – and he's hardly the most reliable of sources – I guess it will remain a mystery. A 'local legend', as it were."

"It will forever be shrouded in mystery," Andy added, a little dramatically.

"Unless somebody tries to shoot Rob again," Charlie said with a smile, in an attempt to lighten the mood.

"Yeah," Andy said, perking up. "And what are the chances of that happening again around here?"

The doors of the pub opened, and Charlie glanced around the corner to see who it was. His mouth dropped open when he saw four tough-looking men dressed in long black coats, all of them eyeballing the room like lions searching for prey. They moved around to the bar, and came face to face with Charlie, who swallowed his concerns and went into his best landlord act.

"Afternoon, gents. What can I get you?"

Andy saw the four men and shrunk into his stool by another six inches.

"Four pints please, Guvnor," asked the tallest of the four men, in a thick South London accent.

Charlie and Andy anxiously turned to each other as the men made themselves comfortable at the bar.

"Can I interest you in our selection of worldwide beers instead?" Charlie said, as much to settle himself down as much as to upsell his beers. He put the beer menu down in front of the men, who didn't even acknowledge it.

"No thanks, mate," the ringleader said. "It's something local we're after."

14

2:21am. 3:16. 3:29. 4:17. 5:02. 5:41.

Rob turned to the clock every time his sleep was broken, and each time his eyes opened, it was in panic. Usually a heavy sleeper, Rob was restless and sweating profusely. His side of the bed was soaking wet, and although Faye would occasionally ask him if he was OK, it was more on drowsy instinct than anything.

Every time Rob closed his eyes, he saw Ray walking towards him with murderous intent. The question of 'would he really have killed me?' was going round and round his head like a hamster in a wheel. To ease his anxiety, Rob tried to work out how many minutes had passed since he last woke up.

45. 13. 48. 45. 39.

It was a fleeting victory, but a soothing one nonetheless.

Sundays for Rob usually started with a lie-in, followed by the football in the afternoon and a kick about with Liam in the garden, depending on how much beer Rob had consumed and how well Leicester had performed in their match. This Sunday was different. Rob decided to take Liam for another walk, in the hope that the fresh air would cleanse him of the evening's events, but also to give him a chance to open up to his son about his past, and the part that it might play in Liam's future.

Liam was happy to be there, even though it was a few degrees colder than it had been yesterday and the geese had chosen to hang out on another island. The swans were mere shadows in the distance, and the ducks had been replaced with a scattering of coots that were swimming in circles and failing to hold Liam's attention.

Rob walked with his hands in his pockets and his head bowed, waiting for the right moment to start a conversation he knew was going to be difficult.

"How are you feeling this morning?" Rob asked, noticing that Liam was as quiet as he was.

"Not bad. Bit cold," Liam replied. He was wearing a Leicester City hat, scarf and gloves set that his parents had bought him on his birthday.

"It is colder today."

Rob prepared himself for the next sentence. "I wanted to talk to you about your grandparents."

"I know that Roy isn't my granddad," Liam cut in. "He's just a man that Grandma met when she felt lonely after Granddad died."

Rob beamed with pride. He was raising such a thoughtful young man.

"That's right."

"And I know that you weren't happy when they moved to Australia, and that you haven't really forgiven Grandma for that. Is that right?"

Rob was taken aback. He felt like a smug criminal who was being interrogated by a detective who knew far more about him than he realised.

"Yes. Yes, that's right. How did you know that?"

"You don't speak to Grandma," Liam said, bluntly.

"It's a complicated situation," Rob said.

"Why?"

"Umm." Rob knew that this was the time to spill the truth out, and that he had to trust that Liam would understand. He gave himself a second to articulate his feelings.

"After your granddad died, your uncle David and I went through a period of deep mourning. I acted out, got into fights, all that kind of stuff, and David became withdrawn and depressed. But your grandma, she…" Rob paused. "She acted like it was the best thing that ever happened to her."

A pause that lasted a lifetime. Liam pulled his father's hand out of his pocket and held it.

"I realise now that for her, it was," Rob said.

Liam looked up at his dad and gave him a reassuring smile.

"Do you miss her?" he asked.

"Very much," Rob said, without hesitation. "I guess I didn't realise how much until now. I didn't realise how selfish I had been, either."

"It's not selfish to miss your mum. I'd miss Mum if she went to Australia," Liam said, causing Rob to let out a small laugh.

"Me too," Rob said. "But I shouldn't be punishing your grandma for it now. I should be supporting her. She's the happiest she's ever been. I just wish she could've been that happy when she lived less than ten thousand miles away."

A rabbit ran out of the hedgerow in front of them and sprinted across the field. They stopped in their tracks and watched it go.

"What do you think that rabbits think when they see us?" Liam asked.

"Why is that giant hanging around with that normal person?" Rob replied.

Liam giggled.

"Yeah, probably."

Rob led Liam over to a bench, and they sat down together and looked out over the water.

"Now that you've shown me how intelligent and grown up you are, I feel more comfortable to tell you about my father, your granddad, and the truth about him. It's something you need to know about, because it's something I've had to deal with, and eventually, you'll have to do the same."

"What do you mean?" Liam asked.

"When you have a reputation, especially in a small town like this, you pass it down to your kids and the rest of your family, and they're tarred with the same brush. Your grandfather wasn't a particularly nice man. He was a violent man. But people liked him because his public persona was very different to the one that we saw at home, and it's important that you know the truth rather than the fabricated version."

"What does 'fabricated' mean?" Liam asked.

"Umm, good question. Like 'exaggerated'." Rob paused to think of an example. "Like Jamie, when he says 'Liverpool are the greatest team on Earth'. That's fabricated, because Liverpool are rubbish and haven't won anything for years. But because he's in love with them and they have had a successful past, he exaggerates how great they are. Does that make sense?"

"Liverpool are rubbish."

"Yep."

"But it does make sense," Liam said. "Why was Granddad not very nice?"

"Alcohol mostly. But he struggled with the fact that he was very intelligent and talented, but he wasn't prepared to work hard and better his situation."

Rob leant forward to see if Liam was comfortable with the subject matter. Although Liam's expression was puzzled and he was wearing a slight frown, it was more to do with processing the information than genuine discomfort.

"I see," Liam said.

"And he took the frustration of his failure to reach for his goals out on the people he loved, which were your grandma, me and David."

"I'm not going to get married until *after* I've become an astronaut."

"That sounds like a good plan," Rob said. "Are you familiar with the term 'big fish in a small pond'?"

Liam nodded.

"That's what your granddad was like. He had grand ideas and plans, but when everybody in the town thinks you're the best thing since sliced bread, why bother chasing them?"

Liam stared out over the water as his dad continued.

"My dad would go to the pub with a tenner and come home with twenty quid. He was so popular, he didn't need to buy a drink, and he was handy with a pool cue, too. He'd challenge anyone in the pub to a game and bet on himself to win, and he'd clean up. It fed his ego, but it also made him complacent. He was scared that if he left this bubble where everybody worshipped him, he would be laughed at. He was the son of a factory worker, and a factory worker was what he was told he could ever amount to. He would leave the pub at midnight and walk home, and on the way home he'd change. In the pub he was a king, but on the walk home the realisation would sink in that he was a simple family man with a simple job and a simple life. By the time he'd get home his whole demeanour and world view would be soured, and he took this frustration out on us."

"Did he hit you and Grandma and Uncle David?" Liam asked, turning to Rob and looking into his eyes as he waited for an answer.

"Yes, he did," Rob said.

"Because he was angry and frustrated?" Liam asked, trying to make sense of it.

Rob nodded. Liam frowned some more, then looked out over the water again.

"That's a rubbish excuse!" he proclaimed.

"It is a rubbish excuse."

"You've never hit Mum or me," Liam said.

"And I never would," Rob replied.

It was time to change the subject.

"What's your next story about, Mr Writer?" he asked.

"I'm going to wait until Grandma Emails again," Liam answered, filling Rob with dread.

"Oh great!" he said, sarcastically. "Maybe a wombat has been electrocuted or a kookaburra has eaten a small family?"

Liam giggled.

"I'm glad you think it's funny," Rob said.

"Oh, it *is* funny!"

Rob grabbed Liam by the scruff of the neck and shook him, growling like a huge angry monster as Liam's body went rigid and he burst into fits of laughter.

"Well, well, well, if it isn't Snoop Robby Rob!" a familiar voice called out from the walking trail.

Jamie must've been taking his talk of getting fit and healthy seriously, as he and his son Carl wandered along the trail behind Rob and Liam. Rob smiled as he saw his friend, even if he did sigh a little. Liam has less enthused about their arrival, and wanted the meeting to be swift, for the sake of the local wildlife than anything. Carl was approaching, and he looked as mean and moody as ever.

"Alright, Jamie. How's it going?" Rob asked.

"How am I going?" Jamie asked, with a face filled with excitement. "It's me who should be asking you!"

Rob gave Jamie the 'don't say anything' look, and swapped places at the bench with Carl so that he could talk to his loudmouth friend out of earshot of Liam.

Carl's backside thudded down on the bench with all the theatricality he could muster.

"Hi, Carl," Liam said, ignoring his friend's foul mood.

"Here we are again," Carl moaned. "Sitting on a gay bench, with gay ducks everywhere, in the gay cold."

Liam had no response. He stared out over the water, where mist had started to roll in.

"That's better," Carl continued. "I can't see those stupid ducks if the mist is in the way, and Dad'll want to leave quicker. He's a crap driver even when he can see."

Liam wasn't in the mood for such a miserable conversation. He was enjoying talking to his dad and hearing about his childhood. He didn't want to hear another one of Carl's anti-wildlife rants.

Rob and Jamie walked up to the trail so that the boys couldn't hear them. Jamie just about managed to contain himself until they reached flat ground, and then it burst out of him. He punched Rob on the arm and squealed with joy as he recounted what he'd heard.

"You absolute fucking legend!" he said. "Everybody's talking about what happened last night. You got shot at, you nutcase. That's amazing!"

Jamie caught himself, his face suddenly becoming serious.

"Oh, but obviously it must've been awful for you," he said.

"It wasn't as much fun as you and the gossip police are making it sound, obviously," Rob said.

"Mate, you have to admit that it's pretty fucking crazy. We'll be sitting in the pub in thirty years' time, telling the little bastards all about the time you chinned a gun-toting cockney and his mate."

Rob sighed. He could picture that exact scenario, and is sickened him to his stomach.

"The town's buzzing, mate. They can't believe it. The local press are all over it, and I bet the national press will be sniffing around soon. You're going to be a celebrity."

Carl was playing the disgusting game of, almost allowing his spit to touch the ground before sucking it back up. Liam's stomach turned as he tried not to watch, but he couldn't help but be drawn to it.

"So anyway, rumour has it your dad was in another fight last night," Carl said, swallowing his spit.

"No," Liam frowned.

Carl turned to Liam and smiled. He knew that Liam didn't want to talk about it, which amused him even more. Any opportunity Carl had to wind you up, he was taking.

"Your dad's always fighting. I've heard Dad talking to his mates about him on the phone, to me mum, to anybody who'll listen. He loves it."

Liam ignored him. Carl leant forward.

"He's like the Incredible Hulk, your dad."

"No he's not," Liam said.

"Yeah he is."

"Shut up," Liam said, his voice cracking.

"Are you going to cry? In front of your gay ducks."

Liam shuffled to the end of the bench. His fists clenched, and Carl launched towards him and pushed him off the edge. He landed in a small muddy puddle, and Carl burst out laughing.

"You've shit your pants," Carl said, holding his stomach as he giggled away.

Liam stood up and wiped the mud away with the sleeve of his coat. Carl stood up and squared up to him.

"Come on then," he said. "Why don't you hit me?"

"I don't want to hit you," Liam said.

"Why not?" Carl asked, as puzzled as much as anything else.

"What's the point?" he asked, and sat back down on the bench.

Carl stood motionless in a fighting position. He wasn't quite sure what to do next. Then something caught his eye on the water. A duck had skidded to a halt on the water, and it made him chuckle. He sat down on the bench next to Liam and yawned.

"Sorry," he muttered under his breath.

"It's OK," Liam said.

"And I take back what I said about ducks. They're alright."

"It's OK."

"I still don't like swans though."

"Uh-huh."

Jamie was too busy gossiping to notice that Rob wasn't even listening. He had been observing Liam as Carl fronted up to him, and it took all of his strength not to run over and give his son a congratulatory hug for turning the other cheek. Rob knew exactly how he would've responded to somebody getting in his face like that, and he couldn't have been more proud of Liam for doing the opposite.

When Rob and Liam arrived home, Faye had made breakfast for them all. Faye kept looking up from her plate at Rob, as if she was checking to see if he was still there, and Rob caught her glance and greeted her with a smile.

Rob was looking forward to telling her about Liam, and the great things he had said on the morning walk. More than anyone, Faye would be relieved to hear what Liam had to say on the subject of fathers and sons, small town reputations and more.

Liam managed to surpass his record of two American-style pancakes and two slices of bacon – with a large drizzle of maple syrup on top – and had started to scrape his fork along the plate. Faye gave him a disapproving look, and a nod of the head in the opposite direction of the table was enough notice for Liam to leave the table, and he ran upstairs to prepare for his bath.

Faye stood up to clear the plates, but Rob was quick to take her wrists and pull her onto his lap. He kissed her on the neck, then the cheek, before burrowing his head into the back of hers and sighing. Faye comfortingly rubbed Rob's thigh with her right hand, and closed her eyes and she felt his breath on her neck.

"It's good to be alive," Rob whispered.

"How are you feeling?" Faye asked.

"Like I'm on another planet. Like I've been given another chance. Like I've been in a Mel Gibson film."

Faye made a sound that was like a laugh that became a sigh, and she turned her head to face her husband.

"You know that there's counselling available for what you've been through?" she said.

"Counselling?"

"Yes, counselling. Mr Proud Man might need it."

"OK."

The wall had come up, and Faye knew it. Fortunately for Rob, he had another card to play.

"I talked to the boy about his granddad," he said.

Faye was taken aback by this revelation.

"I should get people to wave guns at you more often," she half-joked. "What did you tell him?"

"I didn't have to say much. He already knew. He's a sharp kid," he said.

"That's one down, and one to go, then."

"What do you mean?" Rob frowned.

"I want you to make peace with your mother."

Silence.

Rob pulled Faye close to him, and within a few seconds, his grip tightened even more.

That's when the tears came.

And kept coming.

For the first few seconds, Faye was too shocked to react. She felt stupid and awkward, and with it being the first time she had ever seen Rob cry, she had no idea what to do.

After a few moments, she twisted herself round to face him, and wiped the tears from his face. She pulled his head into her chest and held it tightly, resting her cheek on the top of her head as she contained a smile. She almost felt guilty for taking the slightest bit of joy from somebody else's pain, but for Rob, this was a giant leap forward.

That afternoon, Rob sat down at the dinner table with Faye's laptop, and he called his mother in Australia for the first time. When Maggie came to the computer, there was an awkward greeting between the two, mainly because Rob's face was the last one Maggie expected to see looking back at her. But soon enough, the conversation began to flow, and before long, they were talking about the great times they shared, and Maggie filled Rob in with all her Australian adventures.

Most importantly though, Rob apologised for being selfish and for not understanding Maggie's reasons for making a new life. Maggie apologised for her own selfishness, even if it had saved her life at the time, and by the time they said their goodbyes, they were discussing the cost of flying over for a visit.

Faye had never been happier, and for the first time in ages, she felt like the family had something to celebrate. She sat on the sofa with Rob – with Liam squeezing himself between them – and thanked her lucky stars that they were together, healthy and fine.

"Do you fancy going for something to eat later?" she asked.

"Yeah!" Liam cheered.

"I was asking your dad," Faye said, ruffling his hair.

"Oh."

"Do you really want to?" Rob asked.

"Sure, why not? You've got to face the paparazzi eventually," she joked.

"Where do you want to go? Somewhere in the country?" he asked.

"I don't mind. It depends on how many autographs you want to sign."

"OK, that's enough now," Rob said.

Liam threw his hat in the ring.

"The Black Bull," he said. "I like their chips."

"The Black Bull it is," Faye said, as she turned to Rob and they shared a smile.

Acknowledgements

A huge thank you to my wife for putting up with me, and to my family and friends for being so supportive.

A special thank you to Ruth Keene for encouraging me to keep moving forward with the story back in 2008, when *Somerflip* was a play that no theatre or director wanted to take on. I hope you still have your script!

To the awesome Lex and Hope: Thank you for pointing out the glaring deficiencies in my writing and for helping me appear borderline talented (at a push) with your editing and proofreading skills.

To the people I grew up with, and who influenced this novel: You are some of the funniest, craziest and kindest people I know. I owe you all a beer.

And yes, the somerflip really happened.

I think.

I was drunk.

Read more by Daley James Francis

Walking up a Slide

A potty-mouthed rom-com for anybody who has pined over 'The One That Got Away'

Available as an eBook and Paperback at **Amazon**, and as an eBook at **Barnes & Noble, iTunes** and **Kobo**.

"Aimed at a twenty-something audience, but enjoyable for anyone with a quirky sense of humour and a liking for Brit snark, *Walking Up A Slide* is a lovely shaggy-dog story filled with the sort of man-jokes seen in Simon Pegg/Nick Frost works such as *The World's End* and *Spaced*, with a heavy helping of English custom and silly behaviour for those wanting to explore what it's like to grow up in suburban England."

- Cate Baum, *SelfPublishingReview.com*

Printed in Great Britain
by Amazon.co.uk, Ltd.,
Marston Gate.